# Blue Moon

Anne Bourne

Avon, Massachusetts

This edition published by
Crimson Romance
an imprint of F+W Media, Inc.
10151 Carver Road, Suite 200
Blue Ash, Ohio 45242

*www.crimsonromance.com*



ISBN 10: 1-4405-5576-1
ISBN 13: 978-1-4405-5576-3
eISBN 10: 1-4405-5577-X
eISBN 13: 978-1-4405-5577-0

# Acknowledgments

I would like to thank my family for supporting me and for feeding the "starving artist"! To friends: Brittany, who reads all my sketchy first drafts no matter how terrible and Katy, who keeps me inspired.

To Greg, who storyboards with me anywhere and makes true romance a reality. You believe in me and appreciate my artistic nature more than anyone!

I would be remiss if I didn't thank my editor, Jennifer Lawler, for taking a chance on me and making a dream come true.

Finally, to the readers, thank you for reading the story and I hope it takes you away for just a little while to a wonderfully romantic, exotic place. I hope you can escape for at least a moment!

Xoxo, Emily

# Chapter One

*Dive*, her brain was telling her, but Ephyra stayed above the waves. The Caribbean Sea's currents propelled her upward and the waves cocooned her. Ephyra used her powerful tail to stay above the water's smooth edges and let the rain sweep over her face.

Rain. It was such an amazing phenomenon that she'd never experienced until now. Ephyra was a young mermaid by merfolk and human standards. Her twenty-seven years had given her sufficient time to only crave more learning.

Suddenly, Ephyra felt the rain slash harder at her face, stinging her eyes. Clouds swirled like funnels above her and lightning illuminated the water's fury. The waves started to spin and Ephyra finally gave in to dive under the water. It was oddly silent under the waves and dim under the storm's darkness. She swam easily toward the funnel under the water where a strange purple beam lit it up like a candle.

Other fish and sea life were hiding in their rocky shelters. Ephyra was further out than the coral beds, and she saw only a few shadows of larger fish or whales daring to brave the currents.

The sound of a whale's high-pitched cry of distress propelled Ephyra faster toward the funnel. She felt the animal's pain as it was devoured into the purple light.

A black figure emerged, rising like Triton, from the purple funnel. Although he was a merman, his fins were black, split in two and his hair trailed him like stingers of a stingray. He was much larger than normal merfolk and scars ran over usually smooth scales. Ephyra gasped as he reached a hand toward the surface of the water and it parted to reveal the slate gray sky. The creature rose on his massive fins to splay his fingers at the thunder. Lightning shot down and thunder echoed. Except, it wasn't thunder.

Ephyra splashed above the water for a moment to see an airplane—one of those huge pieces of metal she'd read about humans inventing—catapulting from the sky. The winged hull crashed into the water with a reverberating thud. Sirens screamed and lights flashed. Ephyra dove out of the way to watch the plane fall apart like a ghost disappearing under the water.

Two figures, male humans, swam out and sought the surface. The pair made it to the surface, but the waves pummeled them under over and over. Ephyra didn't want to get too close, but she didn't intend to let them drown, either. She was about to help them when the dark merman snatched them up in his fist of power.

They struggled briefly but Ephyra saw the merman, his battle scars running the length of his muscled torso, crush their necks like a handful of sand. A school of spiny backed eels rushed at him like bullets until they surrounded him, and then she heard him laugh.

"Your master has returned."

*Erebos . . . Erebosss . . .*

The shock of realizing whom she watched chilled Ephyra. She retreated hastily for fear he'd see her. Her fins slicked to her sides and she swam for all she was worth away from the Dark merman.

*

"I know what I saw," Ephyra tried to explain half an hour later.

"You're sure it wasn't a Shoal?" her father asked skeptically.

Her mother nodded, but her brow was furrowed. The Shoal were merfolk who abandoned their traditions and were considered rebels.

"It was Erebos. What could have let him rise?" Ephyra swam in small, agitated circles. Couldn't they see that the realm was in danger?

"I don't know. The runes are well protected and no one knows enough magic to have loosed him. Thirty clicks to the south?"

"Yes." Ephyra saw her father motion to several guards and they swam behind him.

Ephyra felt her mother's comforting arm on hers.

"Let's get you something to eat."

"He's too close," Ephyra said worriedly.

"Your father isn't the King of our realm because he's a fool. He will know how to deal with it," she responded kindly.

Ephyra bit her lip. The pleasant memory of the rain was long gone. A slight shock reverberated through the water and made her scales shiver. After nearly a century of imprisonment in the runes, the Dark warlord was on his way. She let her mother take her to her quarters but she kept looking past the rim of their palace.

He was coming.

# Chapter Two

Gabriel Rayner looked at the diving Invicta watch on his wrist. The sapphire chronographs were perfect circles and the metal glinted richly. It was the last thing Charles Rayner had given him, but he hadn't been able to wear it at his father's funeral. Now, it seemed appropriate to wear, when he was the bearer of his father's things to his brother.

"Ladies and gentlemen, this is your captain speaking. We're about thirty minutes from Miami International. In preparation for landing, please turn off all electronic devices, stow your tray tables and return your seats to their upright position. The flight attendants will come through the aisle to pick up any trash you may have collected during this flight. Thank you!" the tinny voice said over the intercom.

Gabriel packed up his laptop with a sigh. He hadn't gotten much work done anyway. He was a professor of English at liberal arts college in a small suburb near Chicago and had the summer off. *One of the only perks except if you're trying to write a memoir,* he thought to himself. Ever since his father's death, he'd wanted to document his father's life if only to keep some part of Charles here on Earth.

The airplane circled for what seemed hours before landing smoothly on the runway. A light rain greeted their arrival. Gabriel shuffled off the plane, avoiding the platinum blond who'd chatted him up for an hour on the flight. She was fit and tanned but not his type. He gave a weak smile as she sidled up next to him.

"Want to share a cab?" she asked with a smile that showed perfect teeth.

"Sorry, I'm meeting my brother," he lied with a polite smile back. She couldn't hide the disappointment and it made him feel guilty. Gabriel sighed.

"Well, if you feel like crashing here's where I'm staying," the blond said with a wistful look. She handed him a card with her phone number and address on it.

"Thanks." Gabriel couldn't think of anything more courteous than that. He claimed his baggage and hastily found a cab.

He was dropped off at the car rental place and pried open the piece of paper that had his brother's number on it. No answer. Gabriel grabbed a map and sat in the Mazda, the new car smell pleasant.

His cell rang and he flipped it open.

"Marcus?"

"Hey! I'm on . . . boat in the . . . got your . . . "

Gabriel ground his teeth. Only his brother would call him on his boat in the middle of a storm.

" . . . was a crash. I'll call you . . . "

"Crash? Are you okay?"

The line went dead and Gabriel wondered if he should be worried. He checked the time and turned the keys. It would be an interesting drive down to the resort one of his mom's friends had recommended. Rain slashed the window and he turned the lights and wipers on.

# Chapter Three

Jake raced in the darkness, his tail silently propelling him faster, deliberately not taking a light with him. He'd glimpsed the dark Shoal army right before a bellow had cut through the water like a mad walrus. Ephyra had been right, the Dark merlord was truly risen.

"Ephyra!" he whispered urgently and peered around the rock wall. The princess was swimming in circles in her coral chambers, and she spun to meet him, her eyes wide pools of gold.

"Jake, he's here. Have you seen my father?"

"He left to find Erebos, but I think he's found us first. We have to get you out of here." Jake grabbed her hand and they swam quickly.

"Your majesty," Jake said and came to a sudden halt at the sight of the Queen rushing down the coral arch corridor. Her sapphire eyes were steely but anxious.

"You two must flee," she said hurriedly.

"You're not coming with us?" Ephyra grabbed her mother's arm and the Queen shook her head.

"If our realm falls to the Shoals, the entire merworld will be overtaken. Go. I will stand with your father."

Jake nodded severely, his duty to protect the princess. In a daze, Ephyra followed Jake through the palace tiers. Ephyra heard mermen guards preparing for war and their grim faces gave her no hope.

Suddenly, the rock walls surrounding them shattered and the castle shook. Ephyra screamed as shafts of rock tumbled toward her. Jake instantly covered her body with his and swam them faster toward the underground levels to a hidden passage that led into Coral territory.

"Jake!" Ephyra cried as a spiny shelled creature with huge green eyes and four arms that carried a pointed spear sprang at them from the windows. It knew how to wield that spear with deadly accuracy, but undaunted, Jake drew his knife to dodge and parry his enemy in flashes of bubbles. The green creature had him cornered when Ephyra grabbed the closest rock, whacked it hard, and the creature floated, dazed. But those huge eyes still watched her, trailing her face. It was one of Erebos' spies, Ephyra thought as she flicked past it.

Down, faster and faster Jake took the princess. He didn't need a light; he knew these tunnels from years of exploring. The Coral people would protect Ephyra, they had only to reach their border.

They wiggled through the tunnels and finally out into open water. It wasn't a comforting feeling. Like most fish, merfolk didn't find it safe to be out in the open, vulnerable to attacks from the sea life. Jake whipped around quickly to see if anyone had followed. For good measure he pushed a large boulder against the opening they'd come through.

They glided over the hill and discovered the glow was from the orange lichens of war. Jake saw the Coral army swimming to meet the enemy with shields, swords, magic flames, and spears of coral. Their small caves were crushed to rubble and green fire sparked across the reef.

"I didn't believe you. I'm sorry," Jake said abruptly, riveting his intense brown eyes on her. She shook her head.

"It doesn't matter."

"It does to me."

"Then, you're forgiven." Ephyra tried to smile.

"I will protect you to whatever ends, you know that," he said slowly, frowning.

"You don't sound sure," Ephyra said and glanced around. The Corals were forming ranks and swimming as a unit.

"I have a place I could take you but you'd have to trust me," he said somberly.

"You know I do."

Minutes later, Ephyra was swimming swiftly after Jake. She paused when she saw a familiar figure cutting through the water toward her.

"Ephyra!" Muriel's voice cut through their conversation. Her eyes were wild with fright and the usually smooth crimson hair was a tangle of knots. Even her fins were paler than normal.

"Muriel," Ephyra sighed in relief as she briefly hugged her friend. Muriel had always been her guide in Coral territory and had become like a sister.

"Has the palace fallen?" Muriel asked in horror. She eyed Jake but they didn't need to take the time for small talk.

"Yes. Jake says he might know a place where we could be safe—you'll come?" Ephyra held out her hand for a friend to take with a firm grip.

"Of course. But if Coral territory isn't safe then I don't know where would be." Muriel turned emerald eyes on Jake, who both fidgeted and looked determined at the same time. "We must go down, deeper than you've been before. You know the legend of Erebos' wife he cast out?"

The two mermaids nodded.

"The sea witch could help us. That's the last place Erebos would look for you—in league with his ex-mate, right?" Jake said in a hurry. Ephyra had never dared go that far down because the pressure threatened to crush her.

"You could be right, but how do you know where she is?"

"I stumbled upon her lair once when I was wandering. It wasn't something I ever intended to do twice," he said with a shake of his head. "But we must hurry."

"Is it better to trust the enemy of my enemy?" Ephyra wondered aloud and then took a deep breath. "Lead the way, Jake."

Muriel's face had gone pale but she followed them as Jake began swimming away from Coral territory. The mermaids flicked their powerful tails and disappeared, while in the distance war torches flared to life and cries sounded the beginning of a new battle.

# Chapter Four

Bikini clad women strutted along the Times Square boardwalk like models and shirtless men made no effort to hide their looks of admiration. There was a lull in the storm and everyone took advantage of it. Gabriel noticed the women but didn't bother to assess any of them. He looked down at his gray suit and white shirt. He wasn't sure why he wore it. Maybe it was because the only time people complimented him on his looks was when he was in it. Or maybe because his father had always insisted that a sharply dressed man was a successful man.

A man in a suit was not an undesirable commodity he noticed, as the women glanced at him. He made his way toward the hotel's open breakfast café. Gabriel chuckled at the thought of taking one of these tanned models home to his mother.

He ate eggs and toast in silence, watching people as they made their way to any number of destinations. The Marquesa Hotel was a quaint resort with a sparkling pool and stucco white siding. His room was comfortable but Gabriel wanted fresh air.

Palm trees swayed heavily in the rushing breeze and even the sea gulls took shelter as the storm began to kick up. Gabriel looked out at the frothing ocean and remembered a time long ago when Marcus had asked their father where the fish went when it stormed. Charles had laughed and said he'd teach them to dive so they could find out.

Gabriel drained his coffee cup and headed for the car. He knew roughly where Marcus lived and found a small parking spot along a marina and went on foot from there, scanning the storefronts for any sign of "Marcus's Dives and Tours." For the next twenty minutes, Gabriel wandered around fruitlessly until finally he ended up at a pier where a man sat in front of his bait shop and read the paper.

"Excuse me, do you know where I could find Marcus Rayner?" Gabriel asked with more patience than he felt.

The man looked up, judged him not a tourist, and nodded.

"Marcus lives back there, number one-oh-two. Not a good day for a dive, though," he said with a grin, revealing cracked teeth.

"I'm not here to dive." Gabriel left the man and went around the back to a white door with a broken screen.

He rapped on it hard to make sure he was heard. After a few minutes, a tousled dark blond head poked out and looked up at him with sleepy blue eyes. The brothers shared that feature of their father's.

"Hey, didn't expect to see you so soon after, you know," Marcus said groggily. He wore only a pair of plain boxers.

"Yea, well, I have stuff to give you and a message from Mom," Gabriel said irritably.

"Huh. Well, I was recruited to pick wreckage of a plane crash a few days ago."

"Congrats."

"A friend of mine is dead." Marcus gazed at his brother and saw Gabriel's face change into sympathy.

"I'm sorry. I'm not trying to be a dick." Gabriel could tell his brother was slightly shaken.

"See you got the watch," Marcus changed the subject, motioning to the Invicta on Gabriel's wrist.

Gabriel nodded absently.

"Yea." He stared at his brother until Marcus seemed to realize they were still in the doorway. He backed up to let Gabriel move in.

"Don't sit on the chair over there. It's broken," he said by way of an invitation.

Gabriel followed him into a dim living room with an adjoining kitchen. A hallway led to what he assumed were two other bedrooms. It wasn't five stars but at least there weren't any roaches like Marcus's last place. His brother wasn't much of a decorator, but Gabriel saw some touches of the female persuasion: a few nice pillows on the couch, pans hanging on the kitchen wall, the neatly organized spice rack.

"So, what does Mom want now?" Marcus called as he popped open a beer. "Oh, you want one?"

"I don't like beer," Gabriel observed.

"So, no?" Marcus shrugged and took a sip. He started making coffee, knowing that was more Gabriel's drink of choice at any given time.

"Mom wants you to visit longer. This hasn't been easy on anyone. She also wants you to get tested," Gabriel said flatly. Their father had been diagnosed with lymphoma several years ago and now their mom was adamant about health check-ups.

"I am perfectly healthy!" Marcus exclaimed with a grin.

"I can see that. Do you always go around half naked?" he asked as Marcus's blue boxers threatened to fall off his slim hips.

His brother wasn't a body builder but a set of six-pack abs poked out against tan skin. Gabriel could understand why Marcus liked Florida, if only for the chance to show off his body in return for female admiration. He self-consciously flexed his own pectorals, wondering if all the hours at the gym were making any difference. Gabriel mainly went there for an outlet when he couldn't sleep, which was more often than not.

"It's too hot to wear much. That's why I love it here," Marcus declared, as if reading Gabriel's thoughts.

"And why are you wearing a damn suit? What are you, forty? You did come to discuss serious business," he chided. Gabriel gave him a small smile.

"It's discounted Armani. And, yes, I came here to sort out Dad's old stuff. I'd hardly call that fun."

The two stared at the floor in awkward silence for a long moment. Gabriel wanted to say so many things to his wild card brother, but from past experience, he knew it would fall on deaf ears.

"So did you want to go through the box together?" Gabriel asked in the stillness.

Marcus shrugged noncommittally. "If you want."

He glanced at Gabriel but his brother was looking around the place and trying to hide his concern. "It's home, ok?" he said preemptively.

Gabriel turned to him with a small raised brow.

"I didn't say anything. I'm glad at least the roof doesn't leak."

They stood in silence again, Marcus sipping on his beer, the sound of the ocean a white noise in the background. Gabriel had a decidedly peevish attitude.

"Ok, well, if you don't want me to be involved I'll go," Gabriel said in parting and turned to go.

"Why do you have to be like that?" Marcus asked in a growl.

"Like what?" Gabriel turned and gave him a steely look.

"Saint Gabriel always helping out the family. Always having to come around and start shit with me just because I choose to live where I do."

"It's got nothing to do with where you live," Gabriel shot back. "You couldn't even have stayed a week after the funeral?"

"So, you're tired of taking care of Mom, I see. Finally, you admit you can't take something anymore," Marcus said with a sneer.

"I didn't say that. I said you could be more available," Gabriel ground his teeth. A slight headache was coming up from behind his temples.

"I was with her when it mattered, Gabriel. You can't say I wasn't," Marcus snarled.

"And when Dad was in the hospital, where were you? And when he asked me to help with a living will instructing them to turn off the ventilator, where were you?" Gabriel forced himself to calm down.

Marcus's eyes were flashing dangerously.

"I don't see how saying any of that matters anymore." Marcus clenched his fists, obviously wanting to slam one right into his brother's handsome face.

"You're right, it doesn't." Gabriel turned on his heel and left the door open.

# Chapter Five

Jake took the mermaids on a plunge so deep, their vision darkened and the pressure crushed their bones.

"How much further?" Ephyra panted as she struggled to make her tail move. She and Muriel were so sluggish down here no doubt because their oxygen was thinner. At least moving generated heat, but Ephyra still shivered. True, merfolk were highly adaptable to freezing temperatures but not for prolonged periods of time. Their cousins in the Arctic had much thicker skin.

"Should be somewhere around here," came the muffled answer. Then they all saw a faint glow of green lights dancing a macabre pattern against the darkness.

"I don't think this is a good idea," Muriel said quietly.

A new, low voice slipped out of the darkness, startling them all.

"Of course it's not. Three young merfolk are quite vulnerable down here," the voice said with a laugh. The tone was at once melodious and harsh, female but with a throaty rasp.

"Scyllane?" Jake asked politely into the gloom.

"The only," the sea witch answered and they felt current running past them.

"We've come to ask for shelter and bear the news that Erebos has risen; he declares war," Jake's voice shook slightly but Ephyra gave him credit for the solid stance he took, shielding her. His magnificent tail was splayed out to make him appear larger.

"Did he?" The woman's voice was amused. "And you thought seeking shelter with me would save you?"

"I thought . . . "

"And what will you give me in return?" Scyllane asked and then, like the furtive manta ray, appeared in front of them.

Her face was pale with luminous purple eyes framed by long, twisting dark hair. A shroud of fins and tentacles cloaked her shoulders down to her tail, which had permanent holes in them. Scars ran in jagged streaks down her tail that caught the dim light when she swayed. Ephyra saw beautiful reflective colors in her scales as the witch held up a light in her hand.

Muriel seemed too stunned to speak. Jake gulped visibly but his face was set in determined steel.

"I'll give you whatever you want. I need protection for Ephyra," he said slowly.

The sea witch swiveled her head sharply to glance at Ephyra. Her eyes seemed to light up and a faint smile crossed her face. She was almost beautiful when she smiled, a fact Ephyra tried to keep in mind as she leaned closer.

"The princess herself, I thought I recognized you," the witch whispered and gave a small bow of her head. Ephyra sensed it was ritual and not out of respect.

"I would be grateful if you could provide us with a place to stay. When the war is over I will see you are rewarded," Ephyra said as confidently as she could. She could feel her parents were dead, the dull ache pounding on her heart. She had to live, had to make sure all that they'd worked for would stand.

"And what makes you think this will be a quick siege? Erebos does not come just for your realm; he will claim the entire ocean. Where will you hide then?" Scyllane asked in a low hiss.

It was a good question that left all three of the merfolk suddenly deflated.

"Come, merlings, this is not a place for discussion," the sea witch said with half a smile.

She turned with a flourish of fins and the three followed. They were led into a cavern of black rock with lichens lighting the interior. The cavern split into several large rooms, some with a curtain of cloudy material hanging over the entrances. Treasures of all kinds lay piled together, with even half a ship that had settled over the roof of the room.

"Where did you get all this?" Jake asked incredulously. He was swimming around like an excited snapper fish as he gazed at wealth.

"A girl can have a hobby." Scyllane smiled at him and offered a ledge for the mermaids to sit. Ephyra did so cautiously as she took in all the amazing loot around her. There were some human things that she'd never even seen before.

She and Scyllane shared a common interest in their fascination with anything that fell into the ocean. Ephyra picked up a few shoes and then ran her hand over some plates. Eating off something round and flat was such an interesting concept, she marveled.

"Now, I would offer you sanctuary, protection, but we all know he will find you eventually." Scyllane surveyed the three around her.

A flat snake wiggled to her and Scyllane let it wind around her arm up to her face. With a startling fast bite, she ate its head. Muriel gagged. Ephyra frowned and turned her head away. Jake merely shrugged, though his fins deflated into a normal stance.

"What's the deal you propose?" Jake asked bluntly.

"Aren't you an impatient one? I propose," she said, "that we make good use of the loophole in the runes."

"So, I'm supposed to go out and find some big monster to save the realm?" Ephyra said with a sigh. "That's a myth. There is no loophole in the runes."

"Says you." Scyllane smiled a toothy grin. "The runes let anyone with enough power claim the throne but you can proclaim a period of time to find a champion to fight for you. Erebos will have to provide his own, of course."

"Don't you think if it was real it would have been written in the laws?"

"Then, why was the slave trade banished?" Scyllane countered. "Countless merfolk had invoked the law to their advantage."

"I can't declare anything, I'm not Queen." Ephyra knew it

wasn't true but she needed to hear it from someone else.

"You are, my merling." Scyllane grabbed a gilded silver hand-held mirror. She turned its surface toward them and they all gasped at the sight of the palace in smoldering ruins. Leech-like creatures were dancing around and all manner of dark sea creatures swam in the mirror's image. They saw the King and Queen's bodies torn apart by the spiny creatures and crabs moving in the scraps. Their crowns floated down to be ignored among the crowd of scavengers.

"Stop it!" Ephyra cried and felt the sting of tears.

"I'm sorry. Your father fought bravely and his wife at his side," Scyllane said and the mirror floated away to sit gently on a ledge.

"How can you know that mirror doesn't lie?" Jake asked in alarm.

"Why would it? Magic does not gain from lies, it is the humans who manipulate it who do," Scyllane explained. "Now, do you want my help or not?"

Ephyra rubbed a hand over her eyes and tried to steady herself. She was grateful for Muriel's hand on her arm, warm and calming.

"I don't really have a choice do I? The merfolk were just beginning to talk about uniting and even revealing ourselves to humans," Ephyra said, faltering at Scyllane's look of disgust for the word "human."

"Yes, humans. They have combed our home very thoroughly and it will only get more invasive. It would benefit us both to help each other," Ephyra said with a grim look.

"So I'll find a champion." Ephyra nodded and shot her friends a determined look. Jake smiled proudly.

"A wise decision," Scyllane said with an almost playful smile. "I will shield you from Erebos."

There was a sudden shift in pressure and the cavern shook so hard, they each ducked from what was surely falling rocks. Ephyra felt a burning in her chest at the high keening sound, like a thousand voices shrieking in agony.

"From a fallen place she will seek,
On burnished heels to spring from light,
His soul of fire to the darkness he shall meet
A slave for the eternal fight."

Scyllane recited the verse from the ancient sea runes while Jake, who knew some of the ancient language, translated what he could. Ephyra couldn't tell if Jake was choking on excitement or fear.

"I'm decidedly impressed," Scyllane said to him and he bowed his head slightly.

"I studied them when everyone else banned them from our libraries. I believe in them," he said to Ephyra. "There are many more verses and I know you don't believe, but it's happening, exactly as it says."

Ephyra had to grin at him. His enthusiasm was endearing to her.

"You always did keep me entertained with forbidden stories. I'll try my best, Jake," she said and gave him a warm look.

She glimpsed a shadow out the window and her heart nearly stopped.

"It's one of those creatures," Ephyra shouted and backed up hastily. Jake grabbed a gold sword and brandished it bravely in the direction of the thing.

Scyllane took matters into her own hands as she shot lightning bolts of magic at the many-eyed creature until it let out a shriek and plunged into the darkness.

"He knows. It's time," Scyllane said quickly. Her face was like marble, pale and flawless. Her cloak of fins now spread out to reveal tentacles under them, stretched in webbing. Jake reflexively stood in front of Ephyra, blocking her view.

"You won't hurt her?" he asked firmly.

"I will hold up my bargain, have no fear. You will have one week," she said and gave a throaty laugh.

An explosion of purple bubbles shot past Jake to Ephyra as the sea witch encased the remaining royal mermaid in its shroud.

The last thing she heard was his scream of "Ephyra!" as she was lifted in a cage of violet light.

## Chapter Six

Gabriel felt the storm explode and still he sat on the bench. His short hair was slick with rain and his suit was now black. It was almost therapeutic to sit and breathe in the fury. He knew he shouldn't have lost his temper but the strain of being alone finally got to him. Thunder crashed overhead and jagged streaks of lightning sizzle into the water. The waves seemed jolted to life as they heaved on the shore.

A few boats tied to moorings in the harbor were tossed like toys on the white caps. Gabriel sat for what seemed like hours and let the wind wash his memory, the rain mingle with his frustration.

The storm began to slow as a few rays of sun poked through the clouds. He saw a flash of movement out of the corner of his eye, and Gabriel turned to scan the line where the horizon met the ocean. The thing was flailing in a way that seemed distressed. He squinted harder into the cobalt water and saw an arm. Gabriel stood quickly, his heart pounding.

*Was* that an arm? He stepped off the pier to run down to the sandy shore for a better view. Was that a head bobbing or was it a buoy? No, it was a human head. He shrugged out of his jacket and kicked off his shoes. With a bounding leap, he dove into the surging water and breast stroked his way out to where he last saw the silent cry for help. The waves pulled at his shirt and crested so high, several times he lost sight of his target.

At last, he reached spot and discovered a young woman with long black hair whose swimsuit seemed to have gone missing. Her eyes were wide with confusion and she choked on the salt water.

Gabriel didn't have the breath to speak so he simply grabbed her and wrapped her arms around his shoulders. The salt stung his eyes as he struggled with the waves that crashed to their backs. Thankfully, they were actually propelling them toward the beach. Still, it seemed to take hours before Gabriel touched bottom and could lift the woman in his arms.

He set her down on the sand and tried not to gaze at her naked body. Firm, high breasts thrust with each ragged breath and brushed his hand. Gabriel instantly jerked it back. He found his eyes wandering lower to a v-shaped waist and long legs that lay entangled together with seaweed.

Gabriel mentally slapped himself and cradled her head. His gaze refocused on her pale face with golden eyes framed by long, dark lashes. She seemed very confused as she glanced frantically around at the land.

"Are you okay?" he asked while unbuttoning his shirt. Even though it wouldn't do any good for dryness he wanted to cover her.

The woman didn't speak but nodded at him with intensely wide eyes. Her gaze traced along his jaw and then to his eyes. She then looked down at herself and Gabriel thought she was going to faint when she saw her legs.

"Hey, stay with me."

The woman tried to speak but all that came out was a gurgle. She cleared her throat and tried again.

"I'm fine," she said, her voice was hard with anger. She tried to stand and then let out a string of curses that Gabriel wasn't even sure were English.

"Are you okay?"

The woman glared at him.

"Do I look okay? I'm on *land*!" she shrieked. "How am I supposed to find a warrior here? I never should have trusted that witch!"

Gabriel cocked an eyebrow at her and waited until she was done fuming.

"So, who should I call for you?" He held out his shirt for her to put over herself and she looked at him as if he were crazy. Gabriel shrugged it over her shoulders anyway.

"My family's dead and I'm stuck here." The woman sighed. "What's your name?"

Gabriel couldn't help the smile starting on his face. He was used to women who clung to him for help but this one seemed determined not to let him take control.

"Gabriel. And you would be?"

"Ephyra." Gabriel liked the sound of her name and it was one he'd never heard of.

"Well, Gabriel, if you could show me what to do here I can manage on my own after that," Ephyra said slowly, regally.

"Show you how to do what?" Gabriel asked, wondering if she was going to go off again.

"Stand," Ephyra said with a frown as she struggled to gain her footing.

Gabriel swept her up in his arms and set her on her feet. He was surprised it felt so right to have her in his arms for a moment. Before he could explore that emotion, Ephyra's legs immediately gave out. She pushed his arms away and struggled to get up on her own.

"Can I take you to my car and we can get you some clothes?" he asked and she nodded. They shakily made it to the black car and Gabriel settled her in the passenger seat. He pressed the gas but the next second he slammed on the breaks as Ephyra gave a shriek that nearly shattered his eardrums.

"What!" he cried and looked around for anything unexpected in the road. The only movement was the windshield wipers swishing melodically in the rain.

Ephyra's hands clutched the seat belt and seat. Her knuckles were white and she glanced around as if the sky were falling, which again made his lips twitch because it was so contrary to her face before. Gabriel looked at her with wide eyes.

"I didn't expect it to go so fast," she blurted out.

"It's a Mazda," Gabriel joked but at her confused look he continued, "How about I drive slower?" He eased on the gas and the car inched forward.

"Oh, well, this is quite smooth," Ephyra said and tried to relax her grip.Gabriel drove them in an aimless direction for a few minutes, unsure of where he could take her. The obvious first choice was a Wal-Mart to get her clothes. He stopped at the first one he saw.

"You're a size . . . " he trailed off, hoping she'd finish it for him. Ephyra gave him that wide-eyed, expectant look that was beginning to look frustratingly familiar. She turned in the seat and the shirt slipped to the side, giving him a peek at a perfectly round breast.

"Never mind, I'll be right back. Please, stay here, okay?"

"Okay." She smiled at him and went back to pressing all the buttons in the car.

In minutes, Gabriel returned with generic shorts and a tank top. He carefully trained his eyes on the road as she pulled the clothes on, only swerving once. Out of the corner of his eye he watched Ephyra's rapt attention out the rain speckled window. Then, she turned to look at him and the jolt he felt made him look away.

"Would you mind if I took you back to my hotel room? I mean that in a platonic, totally non-kidnapper way. If you don't have a place to stay . . . "

"I do not." Ephyra considered his offer. The silence was slightly awkward as Gabriel drove them toward the Marquesa.

"So, what do you do on land, are there giant beasts here?" Ephyra asked as she fingered the seams in her shorts again before, running her hands all over their soft material.

"I'm a professor, English and well, I'm not sure about giant beasts."

"I see. How nice of her to put me in a place with no monsters," Ephyra muttered to herself.

Gabriel knew there was something off about her but he tried to concentrate on the next step. What was he supposed to do with an amnesia patient?

"Oh," Ephyra exclaimed as they entered the hotel room. It was a modest one bed, one bath and a small kitchen area. Gabriel had the unreasonable thought he might want to upgrade to a bigger suite if she stayed. He shook his head—she couldn't stay.

Gabriel watched the woman as she felt his comforter, then wobbled over to the balcony to watch the clouds hover over the ocean. He had to go back to Chicago in a few days. But something was nudging at him as he looked at her.

# Chapter Seven

Jake was thrown by the force of pressure into the rock wall and the breath left his lungs. He could barely see but knew Ephyra had disappeared. Muriel was screaming distantly. He struggled to move, his tail caught under a fallen stone.

A large black cloud of eyes slithered toward him. He saw individual creatures that looked like eels swimming in uniform, but all their eyes glowed red amber. Jake cringed as they came closer but their eyes just glanced over him. Instead, they moved toward the sea witch.

Scyllane was laughing and crackles of magic sparked from her tentacles. Her fins shimmered in glitters of green and blue like the electrical pulses of squid. The black cloud of eels curved around her.

"Can't face me yourself, Erebos, you bastard," she screamed at the shoal of eels.

The largest eel poked its five-eyed head out of the swarm and leaned in close to the witch's face. Long, translucent fangs stuck out of the long mouth. Scyllane gazed it with disdain.

"Where is she?" the eel's disembodied voice hissed.

"Who?" Scyllane felt the blast of the magic and it rocked her backwards. She shielded herself from most of it and sent her own back into the cloud. The eels shrieked as they burned, but the next minute they had reformed.

"You've grown stronger."

"You've grown into a coward," Scyllane growled.

"You know why I cast you out, whore," Erebos' voice snarled.

Scyllane's face creased into an ugly frown.

"You would believe your sniveling, shit eating, waste of a brother over me," she snarled. She blasted the cloud of eels and they scattered for a moment.

Erebos laughed.

"Bring the princess to me or you will wish I had killed you instead of banishment," he said with authority.

"I exiled myself. The princess is somewhere you cannot touch her," Scyllane said, her head held high.

The cloud of eels disappeared into the darkness as the voice faded.

Jake saw Muriel swim over to pry the rock off his fins. A small trail of blood pooled up in the current.

"Are you hurt?" she asked, her luminous eyes concerned.

"I'm fine. Where is Ephyra?"

The sea witch turned to him with almost tired eyes.

"She is not among the merfolk any longer. I've put her on land to keep her safe for seven days." Scyllane went about fixing the parts of the cavern that had fallen in.

"Land?" Jake shrieked. "Why did you put her there? How will she find a champion now?"

"She has never even spoken to humans before," Muriel added.

"Ephyra has a brain; you two will not be needed to coddle her any longer. She will have to find her champion or we all lose," Scyllane said softly. "Nothing in the ocean has been strong enough before so I put her on land to search there."

"You lying bi -"

"Careful, merling. I vowed to protect the princess, not you. She is safe as I said she would be . . . for seven days at least. You may stay here or I will set you on land to be with her, it's your choice," Scyllane threatened. She didn't want company any more than the merfolk wanted to be with her.

"I'll go. But how do I get back?" Jake asked with a raised brow. He was skeptical the witch would even bring them back.

"That I cannot promise. I haven't found the moonstone that will allow a transformation back," the witch said off-handedly.

Muriel glared at her.

"Fine. I want up then," Jake snapped. He looked at Muriel.

"Maybe you should stay here to help find the stone."

Muriel closed her eyes for a moment. Jake knew she didn't want be on land but no one would relish keeping an eye on a sea witch.

"Ok," she consented. Jake gave her a small smile and a look of respect he knew she understood as her spine straightened and she threw her hair back. "Thank you. Does that suit you, Scyllane?" he asked the witch. She swung around and without warning a mass of purple bubbles flooded his mouth and wrapped his limbs.

"Enjoy your sea legs!" she cried and with a flourish, she cast the spell that shot Jake to the surface.

# Chapter Eight

Two hot showers and a room service dinner later, Ephyra calmed down somewhat and was enjoying the taste of steak and green beans. Her curiosity was overcoming her anger as she watched Gabriel use the fork and knife. She thought she was pretty good at catching on quickly. The phrase *six days* echoed in her head but she was so disoriented it was easy to push back. Especially, when Gabriel was looking at her the way he was now, intent and open.

"So, do you have anyone I can call for you?" Gabriel asked for the second time that day.

"Call?" Ephyra looked up from a green bean. There was no way this man could help her but something was pulling at her to stay with him. She liked the crinkles around his mouth when he smiled.

"I mean, do you have any relatives here that you could notify?" Gabriel asked patiently.

"No," Ephyra said finally. She averted her gaze, all too aware of the intensity of his. She knew what he was seeking but she didn't have anything to give him.

"Well, then can I get you a room here for the night?" Gabriel offered.

"No, thank you. I can manage on my own now. You've been very helpful," Ephyra said with a smile and stood. She started to take off the T-shirt he'd loaned her, leaving her dressed in just the tank top.

"Where are you going?" Gabriel stood, too.

"I think I'll take a walk," she laughed. "I've never been walking. I mean, here, on the beach." Ephyra smiled and headed for the door, intent on finding a giant monster for her champion. She tripped slightly but steadied herself on the doorframe.

Gabriel followed slowly, clearly torn between civic duty and a need to return to his solitude.

"So, you'll be okay, then?"

The human had guilt issues dripping from every word. Ephyra nodded. She tried to look confident—it was imperative she move on before she spent the rest of her life finding out everything about Gabriel.

*

The sand was far too rough on her skin and she longed to feel the cool slickness of water. Ephyra stooped at the water's edge, letting it caress her hands and feet. It felt so good that she ached. She waded in thigh deep and then knelt down to let the water cover her head. It was deliciously quiet with only the pounding of surf and under currents. There was no awkwardness like standing on two legs and walking.

A pair of arms suddenly pulled her up. Ephyra came sputtering up above the water to see Gabriel's angry face staring at her. She was surprised at his fierce expression and irritation burst inside her.

"What the hell are you doing?" he demanded. "I leave you for ten minutes and you try to drown yourself again?"

"I wasn't drowning!" Ephyra said hotly. "I don't need your help."

"This, coming from someone who can barely walk and apparently can't swim. I don't need your body as a headline in tomorrow's news and me as a suspect. Now come back to my room," he said firmly and then added a cursory, "Please."

"No." Ephyra pulled her arm from his grip and stumbled back. She nearly tumbled but was proud she kept her feet under her. "I told you I'm fine."

Ephyra saw his gaze slip to where her shirt was plastered against her breasts. She was unashamed of her shape and dared him to comment on it. His blue eyes had gone darker. No merman would ever look at her like that directly. She didn't want to admit she liked the way Gabriel's eyes made her feel desired, more than she'd ever felt before.

"Listen, it's getting dark and you don't have a place to stay." His tone was softer and his tall frame shielded her.

Ephyra grudgingly nodded. She shivered slightly in the evening breeze.

"I can get you a room or you can stay in mine but you need to sleep somewhere besides on the streets."

"The sand looks fine to me," she said stubbornly.

"The sand might but muggers, drug dealers and rapists are not," Gabriel snapped. He was clearly nearing the end of his patience.

"What are those?" Ephyra had heard of those bad titles being given to humans but they had no reality in the ocean world.

Gabriel sighed. "I was enjoying the whole innocent, amnesia girl thing but this is getting unsafe now."

It was almost frightening looking at Gabriel's tall build and broad shoulders, she could imagine if he really wanted, he could simply force her to do anything. But, there was something about him that told he wouldn't ever need too.

"I'm not trying to scare you. I just think right now you should be getting out of the water and into dry clothes," Gabriel said patiently.

Ephyra was annoyed that humans needed to stay so dry. This man seemed to think it was her number one priority. She shrugged.

"Okay. I will take your assistance for tonight, but tomorrow you needn't look after me," Ephyra acquiesced. She felt a concern coming from Gabriel that was both the same but different from what she felt from Jake. It burned her like fire and for once she wanted to know more.

Back at the hotel, Ephyra took at least an hour to explore the shower in his room. She was amazed that fresh water came from a metal head. It wasn't salty or fishy smelling. The soap made her skin soft and she'd never smelled anything like it.

"The bed's yours," Gabriel said she came out in a robe. He'd piled extra pillows and a blanket on the floor.

"Thank you," she said softly. Ephyra sat down on the mattress and instantly loved the surrounding comfort. She lay down and touched the silky pillows. Her head sank into it and she let out a sigh. If this was how humans slept, they definitely had an advantage over seaweed and kelp.

Ephyra glanced at Gabriel in the dim light and saw he was staring up at the ceiling. She could almost hear his jumbled thoughts. The sharp outline of his jaw was covered with light stubble and she wondered how it would feel. Then, she slapped her brain. She had bigger things to think about than facial hair.

Ephyra sighed. How was she supposed to find a champion on land? Loneliness made foreign water well up in her eyes, and Ephyra touched it with her fingers. She wiped it on the sheets, embarrassed. She hoped the sea witch would come to her dreams and tell her why she was here.

## Chapter Nine

Marcus motored his sixty-foot sailboat out of the harbor and into the open waters. He hadn't slept much the night before and the sky was still looking iffy. He'd canceled tours for the day to go out with his partner, Red, and talk. The water was calmer today and the storm's passing brought fresh debris to float on the surface.

Seagulls circled above, calling to each other. They gazed out over the expanse of cerulean. Marcus had been hearing rumors that Perry Sanchez was after unclassified treasure under the water. He was also a huge collector of marine life. It wasn't so much a hobby as a black market for him. Marcus had great respect for the ocean but he realized now in order to get out from under Sanchez he'd have to offer up something valuable enough for Sanchez to let him walk away.

"Have you ever seen *Architeuthis*, Marcus?" Red turned intense brown eyes on him.

"The Giant Squid, no. I have seen things that I never thought were possible," Marcus snorted. "I thought it was only drunk sailors that saw hallucinations on the water."

"Sanchez will reward you and me enough if we find something like that. I need to."

Marcus nodded, although he wanted to just tell his friend to use a condom. Red seemed to get his wife pregnant every two months, they had four children already. They'd both become involved with Sanchez for money and told themselves the lie that they wouldn't let it drag them down or their loved ones. Marcus sighed and wondered if he should tell Gabriel. His brother was always the responsible one and for once Marcus wanted to get himself out of his own mess.

## Chapter Ten

Muriel backed against the wall and tried not to look as frightened as she felt. The sea witch gave her a small smile.

"I envy your youth," she sighed. "How it must feel to have such option.""I don't really have much option anymore, do I?" Muriel said with a shrug. Her entire world was reduced to hiding in a cavern with a sea witch.

"I won't hurt you, merling. You should not believe rumors," Scyllane said and settled herself on a ledge that was covered in lichen moss. The soft glow made her features seem almost normal and Muriel saw circles under her eyes.

"I didn't believe in any of the old legends. Until today." She kept her gaze on the witch. "It's Jake who's the storyteller, anyway."

"How did you come to know him, being of different clans?" Scyllane asked as she leaned back and then floated a tray of food toward Muriel.

The mermaid eyed it suspiciously but hunger overwhelmed her. Most of it was foreign, but she found she enjoyed whatever was not squirming on the plate.

"I know him through Ephyra. He grew up in the palace with her. We met one day when she had crossed the border and I literally ran into her." Muriel smiled at the memory.

"She introduced me to Jake and it was . . . " Muriel stopped, aware she was speaking to Scyllane and not a friend.

"Oh, don't stop on my account. I know you love him, so let's get to the good parts, shall we," Scyllane said and laughed at the mermaid's horrified expression.

"I don't. He's just a friend, I don't even know him all that well," Muriel tried to cover her surprise. She fidgeted with the end of her fins. They were sleek and looked like gossamer but they were tough as armor.

"Soon it will not be race or clan but simply who survives. Even the king and queen were Shoal and Coral. I was a Coral, you know, before I fell in love with Erebos," Scyllane revealed at Muriel's gasp.

"I know, I hardly look it now. But I understand the thrill of the dark looks, the paler skin. His eyes seem to change from amber to gold, don't they?"

"Yes, they do," Muriel whispered. She loved to look at Jake's eyes. He had been nothing like the warnings she'd heard about Shoal merfolk. Muriel wondered where Ephyra was and if she'd know Jake as a human. If anyone could find her, it was him. Muriel felt beyond exhausted as she quelled that odd, aching in her chest.

"Come, let's rest, and tomorrow I'll show you where I seek the stone."

# Chapter Eleven

"Good morning."

Ephyra opened her eyes to see Gabriel's face floating above her. At once those piercing steel blue eyes made her shiver. As she stretched and sat up, the robe gaped open.

"Let's close this," Gabriel said gently and swiftly he pulled the lapels together. Oh, yeah. Humans liked to cover their bodies. She'd try not to forget that again.

"It is your custom to apologize for such a thing?" Ephyra raised a brow and Gabriel burst out laughing.

"It's a good thing I found you. Now, what shall we do about this situation, Miss Ephyra—am I saying that right?" Gabriel asked.

"Ee-fear-ah," she pronounced it and nodded. "And I'm quite sure I can manage on my own now."

Gabriel cocked his head at her. "What's your last name?"

Ephyra thought fast. Merfolk didn't have surnames. "Smith." That was a name she'd read a lot in magazines.

"Ephyra Smith, how much money do you have to get a cab?"

"I have twenty thousand dollars," she said proudly. She'd collected a bunch of money off ships and careless tourists who dropped their change.

"Where?"

"In a bank."

"Where?"

"Here."

"In the Keys?"

"Yes."

Gabriel regarded her skeptically.

"I don't buy it but I won't keep you here. I have business to do today," he said with a shrug.

His cell phone rang, interrupting them. Ephyra found her hearing was quite adept even on land.

"Hey," Marcus's voice came over the line, worried and almost panicked.

"Are you okay?" Gabriel asked, feeling as if that were the only question he ever asked these days.

"Yeah, I'm fine. I'm glad you haven't left. How long will you be here? Can we meet tomorrow?" Marcus seemed distracted. Gabriel felt his irritation rise.

"I only booked the resort for three days, so I guess I'll be around for a few more," he said flatly.

"Thanks, I appreciate it. I'll call you, promise." The line went dead. Gabriel rolled his eyes and sighed. He looked over at Ephyra, who was eyeing him.

"Brother," he explained.

"Oh, does he live here, too?" Ephyra pulled on the shorts and tank top.

"In this hotel, no. In the area, yes," Gabriel said, not taking her knowledge for granted.

Ephyra picked up a brush and rubbed it over her body and then to her hair. She glanced in the mirror and saw Gabriel staring at her as though he were starving.

"Am I doing something wrong?" she asked imperiously.

"Uh, no, I don't think so," Gabriel responded with a grin. He began fiddling with his phone.

*

Gabriel led Ephyra into a clothes store. The manikins were dressed in flowing, summery dresses and others in tight shorts with shirts. He wasn't a fashion expert but Ephyra's eyes lit up when she saw all the colors. He watched her touch the fabrics and press them against her cheek.

"Hey, I thought you said you were busy!" A female voice next to Gabriel said harshly. He turned in surprise to find a blond young woman glaring at him. Her eyes widened in surprise.

"Oh, I'm so sorry! I thought you were someone else," she said, embarrassed.

"No problem." Gabriel flashed her a small smile. "Wouldn't happen to be Marcus Rayner, would it?" He was forever being mistaken for his brother with their similar jaw lines and blue-green eyes. Gabriel's hair wasn't as sandy blond as Marcus's but in certain lighting it didn't matter.

"Yea. You look almost like him," she laughed.

"How do you know him?" Gabriel saw Ephyra approach with a pile of shirts in her hands. He grinned.

"I'm his girlfriend," the blond said with a shake of her head.

"Oh, hi, I'm Gabriel. Brother," he said and extended his hand.

"Jane."

"This is Ephyra. My, uh, friend," he introduced Ephyra and she smiled.

Ephyra shook the extended hand in a mechanical, almost too perfect way. Gabriel didn't comment and hid his smile.

"Wow, so he didn't tell me his brother was in town. I'm sorry for such a rude welcome," Jane said with a grin.

"No reason to be. I just got here, I'm sure he told you our father died recently so it's a business thing for me," Gabriel said congenially. He saw Ephyra look at him with so much surprised sympathy that he nearly forgot about Jane.

"Yea, I'm sorry about that, too," Jane said, bringing his attention back.

There was an awkward pause as the three of them regarded each other.

"Does your hair change its color?" Ephyra asked suddenly. Gabriel gave her a quizzical look, and Jane laughed.

"Every three months I think. I guess you can see my roots coming in." Jane motioned to her highlighted head. "I have this shirt and love it." She pointed at the pile of clothing Ephyra was holding.

"Women here are clothed all too much," Ephyra said and handed her the shirts while rifling through more clothes.

Jane gave Gabriel a quizzical "is she kidding?" smile and he shook his head slightly and grinned back as she started to try on clothes. It was amazing how her smile could make his waiting seem irrelevant. He was glad Ephyra was now attired in something more than generic shorts.

"How do you like this one?"

She wore short jean shorts and a red bikini top. "I love it," he answered truthfully.

"Thank you for helping me," Ephyra said to Jane.

"Well, guess it's time for my part," Gabriel joked and pulled out his credit card.

"Can I feel that?" Ephyra reached across eagerly to touch the plastic card with the raised lettering.

"I thought you'd have a dozen of these since you have so much in the bank," he teased, trying to coax her brain to remember such an ordinary object.

"I lost them, apparently," Ephyra answered fluidly, with a small smile. He let the matter drop as they walked out with her purchases.

Gabriel was intrigued by her sense of superiority and her rabid curiosity. It was a combination that made him feel more than he was comfortable with.

# Chapter Twelve

Muriel held up the glittering azure jewel in her hand, admiring the thin silver chain embedded into the heart of the small round stone. It glowed with an inner light and seemed to whisper. She felt a shiver through her body as it made contact with her skin.

"The blue moonstone," Scyllane said. "It will give any living being the power to change their shape."

"Change their shape?" Muriel asked, in awe of the power she could feel from the simple gem.

"You could become human with this stone and vice versa," Scyllane explained with a grin.

The two had spent long hours mining the reefs and bottom of the oceans for this gem. It was impossible to miss the sperm whale whose carcass now lay prone on the ocean floor. The poor brute had eaten the stone unwittingly, already crabs and fish were feeding on its fatty carcass.

"What else can you teach me about these grounds?" Muriel surveyed the endless darkness. The pressure now felt normal and her eyes were beginning to adjust to the constant gloom.

The sea witch laughed.

"What I have to teach could take decades, merling. But we'll start with the gem you see here. The moonstone is of ancient magic and thus, only the runes could tell us how to destroy it." Scyllane led the way back to her cavern. Eels and glowing fish parted in their path, flicking to either side.

"What's your plan for Ephyra?" Muriel asked suspiciously, suddenly remembering who she was dealing with.

Scyllane turned to her with a crooked smile.

"Ephyra and Jake are on land," Scyllane answered simply.

The witch glided ahead and Muriel hurried to keep up. Her tail flashed athletically and propelled her forward.

"Where will she find a warrior on land?" Muriel exclaimed. "You don't want her to succeed do you?" There was hurt in her voice.

"Of course I want her to succeed." Scyllane turned sharply to face the mermaid. Her murky colored hair flared around a pale face. "Erebos isn't stupid, if he cannot find her in the water, he will find a way to search the land. Do you know what Erebos did to me before he banished me?"

Muriel shook her head. She watched as Scyllane let her fins unclamp and for the first time Muriel saw scars running down the length of her torso and tail, the scales mangled too badly to ever grow back to their former glory. Muriel saw traces of the mermaid Scyllane had once been, flashes of gold and red in an intricate pattern now marred by ugly streaks of gray.

"He beat me for days. Then he told me to run and had his guards hunt me like a seal. If I lived then I had gained freedom," she whispered harshly. Muriel suspected the memories were still fresh in her mind even after decades.

"I'm sorry." Muriel couldn't imagine a mate abusing her so.

"Don't be," Scyllane barked. "I don't need it and it doesn't help."

"But . . . "

"Hush!" Scyllane went very still, her fins collapsed to hug her body again. Muriel listened and couldn't hear anything. The darkness was unbroken and the water peaceful.

"Follow," Scyllane murmured.

Muriel followed the witch as fast as she could. Soon, though, her breath came in short gasps. She wasn't adjusted to the low oxygen level and Scyllane was quick. She saw the faint outline of their cavern and enjoyed a quick moment of relief before a sudden movement caught her eye.

"Scyllane!" she cried but it was too late. A dark shadow blasted from the right and caught the sea witch in its grip. The witch screamed as it closed over her. Muriel could see flashes of her magic but the shadow kept her locked inside.

A low rumble of laughter made her start. She turned and saw a black figure rising from their cavern. A merman. But he hardly looked like one anymore: spines curved from his back and forearms, his tail was split into many tiers with spikes on the edges, and his face was a mass of hollow angles and jutting chin. The merman wore a glistening crown on his head that Muriel recognized from Scyllane's collection.

"Muriel, is it?" the merman's soft voice asked. She was instantly drawn toward it as if they were linked with an invisible chain. As she drew closer, she could see the muscles in his arms and torso.

"Who are . . . " Muriel stammered, but she knew who this was.

"Yes, say my name, merling," he crooned and reached out a hand to caress her face.

Muriel wanted to shudder, to pull away, but somehow she stayed and let his cold touch feel her skin.

"Erebos."

The Dark lord smiled, showing perfectly normal teeth. Perhaps it was the last normal thing about him. Muriel saw the sea witch emerge from the cloud even as it held her back.

"Finally come yourself, coward!" she spat. Her hair was tangled and more of her fins were split.

Erebos turned from Muriel to gaze at his estranged wife. Muriel saw his eyes flicker with passion for a moment and then to pity.

"Scyllane," he spoke her name like an embrace.

The sea witch stopped struggling at the sound of her name. Muriel saw the flash of deep hurt hidden beneath her rough exterior.

"I realize it's shy of three days," Erebos continued. "But I am impatient. Where is Ephyra?"

His tone was pleasant but neither mermaid was fooled. Muriel clutched the blue moonstone in her hand, hoping he wouldn't notice. She saw Scyllane's mouth tighten stubbornly.

"If you confess your mistake, I will tell you where she is,"

Scyllane said coldly.

"Mistake?" Erebos laughed. "What mistake is that?"

"You cast me out on a lie!" she screamed. Her eyes were wild with fury as they cast sparks.

"I asked nicely once," Erebos sighed. He glided up to her and reached a hand out to touch her forehead.

Muriel cringed at Scyllane's screams. She couldn't watch the witch's body convulsing. Gathering her courage, Muriel gave a power a flip of her tail and shot as fast as she could toward the surface.

"Good girl!" Scyllane's faint yell followed her as she rocketed faster and faster. The water was becoming clearer, easier to breathe and Muriel rejoiced in its power to make her travel more rapidly. She could feel Erebos' anger riding behind her like a current.

She rose without stopping until she saw the sunlight filtering down into the reefs. Muriel barely had time to recognize her destroyed home along the journey. The water was getting shallower as she made her way toward the shore. Taking a deep breath and hoping the trajectory was correct, she launched herself out of the water. It was a strange sensation floating above the water and she could see the sandy beach careening toward her. With a wet smack she hit the ground and with a great flop for extra measure, she lay panting on the beach. Thankfully, there were no humans around her.

Muriel stared at the moonstone still clutched tightly in her palm, and put the necklace on. Nothing happened. She wondered if you had to concentrate, so she thought of the human pictures she'd seen. Then, there was a cracking sound and she looked down to see two human legs complete with feet and toes. Muriel's eyes widened as she wiggled them and bent her legs. The waves lapped at her from several feet away, as if to drag her back. The mermaid tried to stand shakily. For a few minutes, all she could do was crawl away from the water.

Soon, she found her strength and stood. It was amazing to be so tall on land, and Muriel laughed aloud. She made her way toward drier ground with a smile. Ephyra couldn't be far. She needed to warn her.

# Chapter Thirteen

Ephyra hung her head over the end of the sailboat and opened her eyes. The salt stung and she nearly pulled back from the stinging pain. *Human eyes really are weak,* she thought in irritation. Soon, they adjusted and she scanned the waters for any sign of life. Only multicolored fish, sting rays, and reef life met her gaze. They didn't recognize her. Ephyra sighed. She popped her head back up and breathed in air. It really was inconvenient not to be able to breathe under water.

Gabriel locked gazes with her and she knew he thought she was crazy.

"See anything?" Gabriel asked with a smirk.

"No," Ephyra said dejectedly. She didn't try to hide her gloom this time. Hope was fast losing its bolster.

She glanced westward and suddenly sat up straighter. In the distance a funnel of clouds swirled over a patch of water. However, within seconds the clouds stopped spinning and settled into simple rain clouds. As innocuous as it looked on the surface, it was too similar to when she'd seen Erebos first arrived He was certainly up to something.

"I didn't mean to make fun of you," Gabriel said apologetically as he sat down next to her to dangle his feet in the cool water. "Are you remembering something?"

He looked at her expectantly with such soft indigo eyes, Ephyra wanted to confide her troubles—her real troubles. Not for the first time was she aware of Gabriel's nearness and the funny way it made her feel. She stared at the chiseled chest leading to defined abs, and as her gaze went lower, she found curiosity taking over. Ephyra had seen anatomy pictures of both human genders, but pictures didn't do this man any justice. Unfortunately, Gabriel was studying her, too, so he caught her unabashedly gazing between his legs, and she felt her cheeks heat up.

"I can't remember much," she said lamely.

Gabriel's snort told her he didn't buy it, but he let it drop. Instead, he smiled at her as if he were amused before suddenly sliding over the side of the boat into the water.

"Come on, maybe getting your whole body wet will help," he said mischievously.

"I can't swim very well," she said and lowered herself into the water. Holding on to the ladder she idled there.

"I remember," Gabriel responded and swam over to her. He tried to place her hands around his neck but she pulled back with an arched brow.

"I am capable of handling myself."

He chuckled, "Fine."

Despite her words, Ephyra struggled at first to remain balanced. She had to admit that Gabriel's swimming ability impressed her. He glided through the water as if he were a merman.

"If I may offer some advice, kick your legs," he instructed haughtily and she gave him a glare.

Ephyra was surprised when her human body managed to make some headway in the water. The movement was jerky and very unlike her tail but she stayed afloat to breathe. It was a foreign thing to be this buoyant on the surface. She had been afraid of falling heavily under the water, dragged to the depths by legs she still couldn't control on land or sea. Ephyra was reluctant to let go of him but soon found herself dog paddling next to Gabriel.

"Why don't you try the snorkel so you can stay under the water?" he suggested.

Gabriel reached into the boat to pull out a black tube that looked like the letter J and a set of plastic web feet.

"Make sure this part stays above the surface or you'll get mouthful of salt. And the fins should help you with the kicking."

He geared her up with the equipment.

Ephyra was delighted at how the fins propelled her even faster through the water. She had seen humans using them before and had simply thought they wanted to be mermaids. Her anxiety lessened in the water. She knew exactly where they were—near a secret spot she and Muriel often visited to chat. Did she dare look for it to see if it had survived Erebos' attack?

"There's a spot I think I remember," she said tentatively to Gabriel. "Would you like to swim over with me and check it out?"

Ephyra could practically hear his skeptical thoughts. *She remembers a random place in the middle of the ocean?* But she just beckoned him and set off, leaving Gabriel no real choice. He donned his own mask, wiggled the snorkel in place and sunk under the waves. The sun's rays illuminated the coral but instead of shades of colors, she saw only a wide, gray expanse. It was depressing to see such life had been destroyed.

They passed over the patch and the reef returned to normal. Stalks of coral were broken here and there, but the marine life splashed to life in vibrant colors that peeped out. Crabs walked along the rocks, blending in with the décor. Gabriel steered away from a jellyfish that hung suspended, its tentacles spread for a meal.

Ephyra made sure to stay close to Gabriel, telling herself it was only because she feared for his safety. He didn't know the dangers could come from more than sharks or stingrays. She liked watching his smooth, powerful movements in the water and more than once, she caught him fixated on her. Ephyra couldn't deny she liked it. She led him under a cavern and then up through a maze of rock. They popped to the surface in the middle of a cave pool.

"Wow, this is amazing. I didn't think anything like this existed."

Gabriel craned his head to get a better look at the rocks lined in various patterns along the walls—and there were even convenient structures that doubled as small steps. He climbed up on them, taking off his mask.

"No one makes it out here often," Ephyra said under her breathe. This particular cavern was a place that was shielded by merfolk magic. Humans could stumble upon it but they couldn't ever find it again.

Ephyra stayed in the water, enjoying floating. She was shyly pleased at how much he liked the place. The water lapped softly at the rocks and sparkled down in little waterfalls from small holes in the ceiling.

"Wish I had a camera." Gabriel smiled at her.

The sunlight bathed his body and for a moment Ephyra thought he resembled one of the pictures in the tales passed around the merfolk. Head tilted back, hair black with water and muscles ready for action. He took her attitude in stride and Ephyra almost felt bad for dragging him around like a helpless seal pup.

She was about to say something when she sensed a presence to her left. Ephyra looked just in time to see the one of Erebos' spies from her nightmares, its giant eye staring at her and its spiny body slunk in the water. She let out a terrified squeak and began flailing to get out of the water.

Through her screeches, she heard Gabriel's splash as he leaped into the pool to try to drag her out of harm's way. She saw him reach forward for her and miss.

"Don't! It's poisonous!" she shouted.

Gabriel heard her but she saw determination on his face to get to her. He froze for a second in terror as he came face to face with the great eye. The yellow orb, slit by a black scythe-like mark glared at him. Without warning, spines shot out from its sides and scraped his arm. He pushed Ephyra away as it thrashed toward her.

Ephyra saw the creature pulling him under the water; saw the panic on his face when Gabriel realized he was running out of air. She grabbed a rock and plunged toward him. Together they slashed in desperation at the one-eyed monster fish. Blood pooled around them in a hazy cloud. The fish floated to the bottom, dead, but Ephyra saw a shadow of another dart away. Another of Erebos' spies.

Gabriel gasped at the surface and dragged himself up onto the rocks where he collapsed. Ephyra was beside him in an instant, her concerned face hovering over his. She could see the poison already running in his system. He'd be feeling hot and chilled at the same time.

Ephyra carefully examined the deep gashes on his chest and arms. She bit her lip worriedly. The fact he was still alive was a miracle in itself. She wouldn't let it go to waste.

"I'll be right back," she told him and dove into the water again.

Carefully, she searched the reef for the roseate snails. She knew the spy would probably report to Erebos within hours and they still had this little matter of getting back to the boat. Ephyra shook it away—there would be time to do that if Gabriel lived. She shuddered.

A colorful, slow trail alerted her to the snails. She plucked two and kneaded them in her hands even as she swam to motivate their slime production. Thrusting herself up out of the water, she applied them to Gabriel's wounds. Instantly, she saw the color change, the wounds closing, and the inflammation going down.

He was still struggling to breathe and to open his eyes. Ephyra could only imagine the pain he was enduring. Tears blurred her vision, and she wiped them away in frustration. It was such a human thing to do. She found herself rambling, wanting him to know the truth, and the truth was easier to confess while he was half unconscious. Something had snapped in her heart and she couldn't live with herself if she was responsible for his death.

"I've never seen a human win against a Shoal spy."

Gabriel's eyes fluttered at her last words. She watched as he worked to move his arms and legs, muscle shaking under the toxin's effect.

He opened his eyes and tried to smile to reassure her until he became aware of the mass of bites and scratches across his torso. His raised eyebrows said it all.

"They'll heal over and you shouldn't have any scars. The toxins will wear off in a while. But I need to tell you the truth," Ephyra whispered, her eyes full of fear. "I don't have amnesia or whatever it is you think I have."

Gabriel tried again to speak, but his vocal cords were frozen. She saw him probing her eyes with his, wanting to understand.

"I must leave to protect you," Ephyra took a deep breath. "I'm not human. I don't know much about living on land." She tried to shrug nonchalantly, but the gesture wasn't convincing, even to her. "I didn't expect you'd stay with me. I can't let anything happen to you because of me. I'm a mermaid." Ephyra let the words ring out in the cave.

She nearly laughed out loud. "A mermaid on the run actually, I need to find a warrior on land." Ephyra stroked his hair, his brow, knowing it was probably the only time he'd let her.

His eyes were darting all around her face, searching for lies but finding only fact. She held his face in her hands, the better to memorize those indigo eyes, the stubble on his jaw and the wonderful heart that had saved her. The toxin was slowly working its way out of his system but he couldn't yet move his body.

"You know the way out of here. It should be safe for you, but as soon as you can, get back to your boat," Ephyra sighed and leaned down. With a swift motion she kissed his cheek and then splashed into the water. The fins on her feet propelled her down and under the pass to exit the cave.

Her heart was like a compass that wanted to point her back to his side, to feel something she'd only heard about. But her mind wouldn't let it and Ephyra swam as hard and fast as she could to the shore. They hadn't sailed all that far and she reached the beach without difficulty. Their white boat still bobbed in the ocean, anchored and waiting for the next adventure. She had no doubt he would live, but she wondered how she would live without him.

## Chapter Fourteen

Gabriel faded in and out consciousness but finally felt strong enough to sit up. The sunlight was weaker but not quite twilight. He saw the cuts and bites were actually healed and only a faint trace was left. That's when he remembered Ephyra's words, spoken in what he had assumed at the time was a hallucination brought on by the attack.

*Did she say mermaid?* He shook his head. Maybe she did, maybe she didn't. Gabriel had never had slime cure bites before, so could mermaids be far behind? He stood shakily and reached down to retrieve his snorkel and mask on the ground.

*Get to your boat as fast as you can,* her words floated back to him. Gabriel slipped the mask on and gently eased himself into the chilly water. He dove swiftly and left the cave behind. Checking the Invicta, he saw it was nearly the time to turn the boat back in. The sun was sinking into the horizon as he motored back to the harbor. He hoped the rental guy didn't remember he'd gone out with a woman and returned alone.

Gabriel slipped his shirt on, hoisted the bag over his shoulder, and turned in the keys to the boat. The man merely nodded at him. Gabriel flipped open his phone to find three texts and a voicemail waiting. He listened to Marcus's worried voice and sat in his car, deciding whether it warranted going straight over there or going back to the hotel for a shower.

Gabriel conferred with his watch again and saw it was almost seven P.M. He opted for the hot shower first and steered the Mazda toward the hotel.

*How hard will it be to find a woman who doesn't know anything about human customs?* He couldn't dump the thought from his mind as he showered and changed. He also couldn't understand why it mattered so much to him. He'd met her for a few days and now he needed to be next to her, to be the one to expose her to new things?

Exactly forty minutes later, he parked and walked into the dimly lit Hannah's BBQ. He gingerly sat down in a booth, across from Marcus's pale and nervous face.

"Okay," Gabriel groaned as he moved his abdomen. "What's wrong?"

"What's wrong with you?" Marcus asked in concern.

"Nothing." He grimaced. The waitress interrupted any further conversation.

"What can I get ya?" She smacked her lips and held a pad of paper.

"Scotch on the rocks," Gabriel said, in need of alcohol. "And the black Angus burger, medium rare."

"You ready now, hun?" She turned her attention to Marcus.

"Same burger, thanks."

She walked away and Marcus turned to his brother.

"Look, I'm sorry about the fight . . . "

"Wow, was that an apology?" Gabriel cut him off sarcastically. Marcus only smiled, refusing to take the bait.

"Sure. I know I should be more responsible, I get that. But I'm in a bit more trouble than I can handle at the moment," Marcus swallowed apprehensively.

"Funny, it seems to hit us both down here," Gabriel reflected.

Marcus noted his brother's drawn face and the scratches on his face.

"You go first," Gabriel said as he finished the Scotch.

Marcus gulped. "I made a deal with a man named Sanchez, yes, he's a drug lord and yes, I realize I am a retard. My partner pretty much just sold me out a few hours ago."

Gabriel eyed him with a raised brow. He accepted the scotch from the waitress.

"Okay, and?"

"And my partner, Red, told him we could find whatever Sanchez is looking for. He expects the job to be done and I can't do it." Marcus blew out a frustrated breath.

"You owe him money, don't you? How much," Gabriel asked wearily.

"More than I'd ask to borrow."

"What does this Sanchez want?" Gabriel watched his brother roll his eyes.

"He wants anything unusual from the sea, probably a damn mermaid," Marcus said and snorted sarcastically.

Gabriel glanced at him sharply to see if he was kidding. There was no way Marcus could know about Ephyra . . . he felt his heart beating faster.

"And why does he think you can find one?"

"Because I've found half the dives around here and remember Australia? I got written up in a book for that one," Marcus said with a small grin. He sobered quickly. "Remember dad used to say they were around if you looked hard enough?"

"I found a mermaid," Gabriel said suddenly, unable to keep the words from pouring out of his mouth. He wanted to try them out loud and see if he believed it anymore. He instantly regretted it when Marcus' eyes lit up and he learned forward.

"No shit." Marcus stared at him as if he'd just won the lottery. "Are you in on this or something?"

"I wondered the same thing. But you didn't know about the woman I saved from drowning right?"

"Really?"

"Didn't think so. But it doesn't matter, she left and I probably won't find her again," Gabriel said, aware of the angst in his voice.

"I need you to find her." Marcus was like a shark now and Gabriel frowned.

"I wouldn't give her to you even if I knew where she was, Marc. I only have her word she's a mermaid anyway."

"Sanchez is a drug lord who will kill me, is that what you want?"

Gabriel heard the fear in his brother's voice. He ran a hand over his face and sighed.

"He'll kill Jane, my girlfriend and maybe he'll come after you, too, I'm sorry. I fucked this up but I just need to show him she's real. I won't 'give' her to him," Marcus said pleadingly.

"Yea, I met Jane, she seems nice. Mistook me for you."

"I love her, Gabe. Please, help me. I know I don't deserve it but I want to walk away from this."

Gabriel hadn't ever heard his brother say he loved someone other than himself. He looked into Marcus' eyes and his heart clenched painfully. He didn't want to share Ephyra with anyone, no matter the consequence.

"If I find her, I'll ask her." He left it at that.

They paid for their meal and as they walked out of the restaurant, the sound of shocked gasps drew their attention. Surely, this was another dream: a naked woman, this time with long burnished red hair, walking along the beach toward the dinner crowd seated an outdoor cafe. Well, she wasn't completely naked — she wore a smile and a necklace.

He groaned while Marcus whistled in that cocky way all males had in the presence of female nudity. At least in the darkness the shadows covered her.

"Hey," he called and the red-haired woman turned to him. Her eyes showed some fear and Gabriel slowed his rush, not wanting to resemble a charging bull.

He whipped off his shirt for the second time in as many days to cover an unclothed woman. She didn't complain as the material settled over her upper half.

"Oh, thank you," she said pleasantly curious.

"You been working out?" came Marcus's annoying observation. Gabriel gave his brother a sarcastic glance and turned back to the situation.

"What's your name?" he inquired of her.

She turned brilliantly green eyes on him. She was just like Ephyra in that wide-eyed, innocent amnesia patient kind of way.

"Muriel."

"Okay, Muriel, did you come from the ocean, too?" Gabriel asked as he steered her toward his car.

"How did you know?" Muriel exclaimed. "A guess." He smiled. "Can I take you back to my hotel room and get you some clothes." It was not so much a question as a command.

"I don't need help, thanks," she said and made to move off.

Gabriel growled under his breathe, reaching his limit with proud mermaids and put a firm hand on her shoulder and steered her toward the hotel lobby.

"I need you to help me find Ephyra."

"You know her?" Muriel asked excitedly.

"I did," he said pointedly but didn't elaborate as she gave him a quizzical look.

The brothers hustled Muriel into a large foyer, which she gazed at in awe, then into an elevator before shuffling down a hallway to room 315. Gabriel noticed she was just as amazed that a plastic card opened the door as Ephyra had been.

"I need to speak with Ephyra immediately!" Muriel said with as much haughtiness as she could muster. Marcus followed and closed the door.

"I would speak with her myself, if I knew where she was. Are you telling me you don't?" Gabriel asked menacingly.

He was in no mood to play games. Marcus put a hand on his shoulder and motioned him back a few steps. Gabriel acknowledged and fell back.

"What?" he hissed, keeping an eye on Muriel, who did the same inspection of the room as Ephyra had. Gabriel felt something in his breast tighten.

"What are you doing! Do you know this woman?" Marcus whispered urgently.

"I know her friend. The mermaid, okay?"

"You said you lost her."

"She left me."

Marcus laughed. "That's a first."

"Shut up."

"I have an idea." Gabriel went to stand in front of Muriel, who was gazing through the glass as if she'd never seen the ocean before. Or, perhaps, she'd just never seen it from this side.

"I know Ephyra's a mermaid, I didn't want to believe it but now she's in more danger because she left me and might run into people who won't be as nice as I am." Gabriel left the threat open ended.

He felt Muriel's intense gaze, as if she were reading his thoughts. She put a hand to his chest and he instinctively backed away. She smiled up at him.

"What is your name?"

"Gabriel."

"I think you have more than a kind interest in her," Muriel said with a laugh.

Gabriel saw his brother smother a grin and a cough.

"I don't think that matters. You two don't get the danger you're in here."

Muriel just smiled at him and nodded. "I will help you."

## Chapter Fifteen

Ephyra wandered listlessly along the streets, not caring that her hair was tangled or if there was dirt on her face. She had combed as much of the city as she could looking for anything to tell her how to find a champion.

She found herself now wandering back at the shoreline with the waves crashing along the sand. Twilight had set in a dying blaze of light. Clouds marred the fading light and streaked across the sky like phantoms. Ephyra tried not to feel homesick. She wondered if her parents could see her from the afterlife. She wished they were here now to help. Her time was running out and she was upset that all she'd done was fall in love with a man who could never be with her. Had she just thought love? She sighed.

A familiar figure was walking along the beach ahead and Ephyra almost fainted. Muriel? She called out to her but the woman continued walking until she was joined by a tall man with blond hair. Ephyra began to run after the pair, certain it was her friend. People crowded her way as she ran forward.

She forced her legs to go faster but she wasn't sure-footed enough yet to go very quickly. Ephyra tripped and fell into someone's arms. She hadn't even seen the man as he caught her. Something about the way he held her possessively made Ephyra shiver.

"Gabriel?" She looked up at piercing blue eyes that held a hard stare. Gulping, Ephyra glared back at him hoping it would make him back off.

Gabriel didn't slacken his grip as he pulled her to the side of a grove of palm trees. It was growing darker as he pushed her up against a tree. The hum of insects assaulted their ears.

"Were you ever going to see if I made it out alive?" His voice was cold but Ephyra heard the hurt in it.

"I didn't want to hurt you. You'd already helped," she stammered. The pair was long gone and Ephyra sagged against the rough bark of the palm.

"Really. So I risked life and limb to save you for you to leave?" Gabriel leaned in closer and Ephyra could feel his warm breath on her cheek. She twisted sideways but he caught her. His grip burned like fire and he firmly held her without much effort. Ephyra glanced up again at his angled jaw and tight lips. She knew it wasn't physicality that held her here.

"I needed to get out of the water." It didn't seem to appease him; she wondered what could.

Ephyra stilled in his arms as he leaned closer. She could smell his cologne mixed with the headiness of the sea. His white shirt had two buttons undone and she could almost see his heart beating. She certainly heard it. The air was inflamed with liquid heat. It was her turn to feel the breathless out of control fire that she had to acknowledge as passion.

"You kissed me without permission," he said in a low growl and his lips came within a breath of her cheek. Ephyra felt a shiver go up and down her arms. She turned her head toward him this time.

She was painfully aware of his close proximity, how his chest breathed in and out. It touched hers, skimmed her breasts to make her feel warmth she'd never experienced. There was something in this human body that longed for release, for escape. Ephyra wasn't sure what.

Gabriel thrust his hips into hers and locked her into place. Ephyra suddenly felt electricity shoot through her skin and between her legs. She saw his eyes roving hers, a wild excitement in them, a restraint he'd been keeping in check. He moved away and Ephyra didn't like the coolness he left. She unconsciously moved toward him to bring him back and it was all the invitation Gabriel needed.

With a fierce, low groan he plunged onto her mouth, capturing her lips. Ephyra sighed and sank deeper into his body, feeling his muscles tighten. She moved her lips slightly to part them and felt his tongue reaching gently toward her. She was barely aware of the coarse bark of the palm against her back as his body pushed into her. Gabriel's hands wound more tightly around her and the kiss deepened. Ephyra's breath was gone, she couldn't think straight, and her new legs gave out.

Gabriel laughed wickedly as he felt her weight crumble. He followed her to the ground and lay over her. Ephyra reached up to push at his chest but stopped when she felt his pulse there. It was right, it was simple.

"Unnhh." Ephyra didn't know what was raging inside her body but it was happening too fast.

Gabriel saw the fear on her face and instantly backed away. He rubbed a hand over his face, trying to snap himself out of the moment. A moment more and he'd have had her on the beach in front of who knew who was watching. He held out a hand to help her sit up. They sat facing each other for a silent minute.

"I don't know why but I need to be with you. Don't leave again," Gabriel said softly.

Ephyra saw him smile through the dim light and the wind leafed through his hair like invisible fingers. The smells of sand, salt, and his cologne framed the perfect picture of his sharp profile.

"I can't promise that but I'll always say goodbye," she said and wondered how much more she wanted to know. It wasn't simply physical, her emotions felt as if they were in a riptide. She knew she couldn't encourage this love, Gabriel could never be with her.

He seemed to accept her answer for now and led her toward the quiet ocean front café where Marcus and Muriel sat waiting patiently on the couple. Ephyra gave a shriek and the two hugged each other exuberantly.

"How did you get here?" Ephyra exclaimed and then glanced at Marcus.

"Ephyra," she said and held out her hand to Marcus in an effort to uphold all human customs. He smiled widely at her.

"I'm Marcus, Gabe's brother."

Ephyra could see the Rayner resemblance in the startling blue eyes. Gabriel grabbed the chair next her at the small wooden table.

"I'm so glad you're all right, my lady," Muriel rushed ahead, her eyes never leaving Ephyra's face.

"So, how is this form possible?" Ephyra asked curiously.

"Scyllane, of course. We found the blue moonstone," Muriel said in a whisper and motioned to the necklace she wore. Ephyra gasped in delight.

"Erebos caught us though, and I'm afraid for Scyllane. I shouldn't have left her but I needed to find you. We don't have much time left, he's destroying the realms and we need you to find the champion," Muriel said as tears began trickling down her cheeks. She looked down in surprise.

Ephyra handed her a napkin. "It takes some getting used to," she said gently. "I'm glad you're here. Has Scyllane given any clues why I'm here? What champion could I possibly find on land?"

Gabriel and Marcus exchanged inquisitive looks with each other but remained silent, listening.

"Where is Jake?" Ephyra frowned, wondering why her friend would leave Muriel alone with the witch.

"He's not here?" Muriel sighed. "Scyllane sent him to be with you so I thought you'd know."

"Wait, there's another naked mermaid, er, merman, out there?" Gabriel interjected.

"Jake was an orphan who warned my father of an attack. He's lived in the palace with me ever since," Ephyra explained. "We have to find him."

"Excuse me, palace?" Gabriel asked in surprise. Ephyra grimaced. She had hoped he's miss that word.

"My home," she said hesitantly. "I'm the daughter of the late king."

The silence was palpable.

"So you have ranks among mermaids?" Marcus asked abruptly and Gabriel continued to look shocked. Ephyra sent him a plea of understanding in her eyes and he ran a hand over his face, whether from embarrassment or anxiety she wasn't sure. She could tell her being royalty had changed the way he looked at her but she desperately wanted it not too.

"We have a governing system like you do, but we grow to adulthood in about thirty years and then it slows. Our eldest is over six hundred years old," Ephyra explained.

"Wow." Marcus smiled and tapped his fingers on the table.

Ephyra noticed that though Marcus smiled, he seemed preoccupied and expressly interested in her. Sometimes she caught him staring at her as a young shark eyed a school of fish.

"We should find a different place to eat, I'm sorry, this is so backward," Gabriel muttered and half stood. She placed a gentle hand on his and pulled him back down.

"I don't need to be treated differently, please."

Gabriel regarded her for a serious moment and then sighed. Ephyra was relieved that he didn't move away but she could feel the uncertainty in him.

"So, we're all on land," Ephyra groaned. "That doesn't help anyone in our realm."

"We need to find Jake, he'll know what to do," Muriel said with a nod.

"Well, until such time, I think we should eat and then I need to run," Marcus said vaguely.

Ephyra saw him glancing around nervously at the other patrons. She wondered what was making Gabriel's brother so anxious. He seemed to be a polar opposite to his brother.

Then, a large posse of men approached their table and Ephyra felt a shiver go through Marcus.

# Chapter Sixteen

The palace was just as he remembered it. Erebos trailed a hand along the alabaster decorations and the rock walls. Twisting halls and high ceilings ornately reined over the rooms. This room was his favorite, though. He entered the large, rocky cavern filled with slabs of stone, chains, weapons, and all sorts of restraining equipment. He was familiar with all of it because each piece had been used on him at one time or another. Now Erebos was the wielder and not the prisoner. He had heard rumors that the recently deceased king and queen banned this room. He shook his head at their stupidity. If the merfolk did not have a healthy fear, there would be no rule.

Erebos studied the witch's prone body, her head sagged and the old scars covered by new wounds. What a waste. Scyllane was a talented mermaid but she had chosen to betray him.

"I know you have something that will let me find Ephyra. Is it this?" He held up a treasure box with ancient symbols.

Scyllane forced her head up and glared at him. He'd ransacked her cavern and brought her treasures to the torture room. There were several that contained magical powers. He watched her closely to see if anything sparked her interest.

"Then it's worthless," Erebos snarled and with a snap the box exploded.

"If it gives you pleasure to destroy my things, may I at least be offered a more comfortable seat to watch?" Scyllane hissed. She strained against the chains that held her like a crab trap. Her magic was waning with her strength.

"So you did bring her back," a new, male voice interrupted them.

Erebos turned to see Sevag, his brother, entering. His long tail had only half a caudal fin and his scales were odd patches of gray and green. Sevag was truly an ugly beast.

"Of course I did," Erebos said and clasped arms with his brother.

"Just like old times, huh, Scyllane?" Sevag swam close. Erebos always admired his brother's penchant for invading others' space—it stripped their comfort and often produced better results than outright torture. He also knew Sevag had an eye for whatever was his, including his mermaids.

"You're prettier than I remember," he whispered into Scyllane's ear. She turned her head in disgust. Erebos could imagine his breath stunk of rotted fish.

"Lying son of a bitch," she spat and flicked her tail so that it slapped his away.

Sevag laughed and turned to his brother.

"She still has that spark."

"Indeed," Erebos said and continued to sort through her stash of treasure.

"What do you need all her crap for?" Sevag asked as he touched the mirror. He held it up and studied his scarred face in its reflection.

"Humans have the greatest things," he said giving himself a sharp-toothed grin.

"She uses something to spy on the realms and I need it to find Ephyra." Erebos held up a glittering staff for Scyllane. She shook her head and the staff splintered.

"That little half-breed princess?" Sevag smiled. "Has she grown, now? I wonder how she turned out."

"Nicely. I will give her a choice, Scyllane. Surely, you didn't think I'd kill her without offering something for her life?"

Erebos saw his ex-mate eyeing his brother playing with the mirror intently. She turned to him with a sour expression.

"She won't be your partner, and you're wasting your time looking for her," Scyllane said wearily.

"The lost mermaid princess goes down into legend, and I will be called tyrant? I think not," Erebos said softly. "She will make history with me or die."

Sevag lost interest in the mirror and leered at Scyllane and licked his lips. He sidled up to her again and ran a cold hand over her breast. Scyllane shifted, and he knew she was carefully stifling her fury.

"Do you think she's still fertile?" Sevag asked his brother. He tossed the mirror to the side and Erebos saw Scyllane's eyes track it.

"I don't care, and I'm sorry I don't," he said. They had planned such a future together until the bitch betrayed him. He could feel her pain, too.

"I'll check for you just in case." Sevag leered at the witch.

"It matters not," Erebos said.

For a moment he thought about stopping his brother. But the painful memory of his wife's lies had killed his last desire for belief in innocence.

Erebos watched as Sevag took his time groping her body. His touch was gentle sometimes as he caressed Scyllane's breasts and down her tail. Then in a terrifyingly slow pull he tugged her scales out. Scyllane muffled her screams, not giving him the pleasure. Erebos smiled sadly—she would have made the best queen.

Sevag finally grabbed her tail and peeled away the scales at a small spot. Scyllane writhed to get away, her cries now unleashed. He stuck a finger in the delicate pouch there and laughed.

"I'd hate for there to be more traitorous bitches made," he said in a cruel whisper.

With agonizing slowness he dug his nails in the inside of her egg pouch. Scyllane screamed. Erebos felt breaking in some part of him he'd thought was dead. He left before he had to watch Sevag pop the eggs that came floating out. He swam hard and fast to get away from it.

## Chapter Seventeen

"Marcus Rayner."

Marcus beamed his best bullshitting smile at Perry Sanchez's dark-skinned face. The drug boss was dressed in a lightweight suit with shiny shoes and three of his men behind him. They wore the same expression: causal, but effective, bodyguards.

"Good evening, Mr. Sanchez. I was just going to call you," Marcus said with a nervous tick. He stood.

"And who are these enchanting young women? Manners, Marcus."

Marcus wondered if his boss could detect at first glance how different they were, but he introduced them anyhow. The mermaids nodded at the acknowledgement, but quickly slid their gazes back to their plates. "Can I have word outside, sir?"

Marcus was relieved when Sanchez nodded and bade everyone a good evening before leaving the restaurant, never looking to make sure Marcus followed.

"You have found them?" Sanchez was always direct.

"No, sir. But—"

"Red tells me you can find mermaids."

"Umm . . . "

Marcus tried to still his nervously tapping toes. The drug boss looked like a praying mantis sizing up his meal.

"But how much will I owe you to forget Red said that?"

Sanchez shook his head, his big hat bobbing. His men chuckled at Marcus' nervousness.

"How much will you not like me if I dispose of your girl and your partner if I don't see a mermaid?" Sanchez asked jovially.

Marcus sighed. He had seen the look on Gabriel's face when he'd looked at Ephyra. There was no way he would convince him to even involve her in a plan with Sanchez.

"All right, tomorrow night, at the bay, okay?"

Sanchez smiled broadly and motioned for his men to move away with him.

Marcus glanced in the restaurant window and saw Muriel. Perhaps it was time to put his charm to the test.

## Chapter Eighteen

Erebos finally went back to the torture cavern. He stared at his prisoner for with a heavy heart. He wanted to have Scyllane at his side, to remember the way she laughed at his wit. Instead, she watched him with murder in her eyes.

He glanced at Sevag, who was chuckling to himself.

"Enough!"

Sevag gave him a disgruntled look but exited the cavern with a swish of his long tail.

"My hero," Scyllane croaked, still strong enough for sarcasm. "But still only willing to believe what he sees, not what he's told."

Erebos sighed. He had loved her more than the tides loved the moon. Still, it was a great punishment for mermaids to have their eggs taken and not something done lightly.

"Scyllane," he started but then stopped. It was over now.

He scooped up the mirror his brother had played with and saw his dark reflection. When had his eyes become so black? His hair gray and scraggly like seaweed?

Suddenly, the mirror hummed to life. Its surface sparked white and then ran a series of images of two merfolk he didn't recognize.

"Who are they?" he asked and held up the mirror to her face.

Scyllane eyed it warily and he realized she was losing control of her magic. That could have been the reason the mirror hadn't responded until just now.

"Jake. The orphan the king rescued. I do not know this other mermaid. Why can't I see Ephyra?" he demanded and held the mirror up.

Scyllane smiled blandly.

"Why can't I see her?" Erebos repeated to himself, knowing the sea witch would not help. "There is magic of some sort she's found."

He glanced back at Scyllane and his eyes sagged for a moment in grief. He kissed the tips of his fingers and tossed it to her.

"I fear I won't see you again, pet," he said and in a sweep of bubbles was gone.

# Chapter Nineteen

"Hey, Muriel," Marcus said as he walked up behind the red-headed mermaid, as she sat on the sandy shore. It hadn't taken much to persuade Gabriel to take Ephyra somewhere for dessert and he'd promised to look after Muriel.

She turned with an eager expression, long auburn hair cascading off her shoulder. For a moment, Marcus hesitated in what he was about to do. The blue stone necklace sparkled between her breasts. He drew a breath. *For Jane and a new life after this is over.*

"Hello," she said.

Marcus saw her interest in his tanned body and wondered if seducing mermaids was like women. She was staring at him with interest so he played on that, keeping his shirt off and lightly brushing her as they walked.

"So, how are you doing? Adjusting okay?" He grinned.

"Yes, thank you, walking is harder than I thought. You are talented," she said with a smile.

"I suppose so. Would you like me to show you around the Keys?"

Muriel hesitated and Marcus waited patiently. What better time to win her affections than when she was longing for someone to look at her the way Gabe did at Ephyra? It was sneaky, but Marcus couldn't let Jane come to any harm and this opportunity was waiting for him all tied up with a bow.

"Sure, that would be nice." Muriel took Marcus's outstretched hand and he helped her stand.

The night air was softly humid and sweet scented. He watched Muriel listen to the wind and waves with a curious expression. The moon hung at half-mast in the sky and illuminated the water.

Marcus wondered if Muriel thought Florida was dry compared

to living under water. She walked along easily, her stride long if a bit hesitant.

Marcus steered her protectively around sand castles and holes kids had dug. "So, do you like it up here?" Marcus asked with a twinkle in his eye.

Muriel laughed.

"I like it, but I'd never get used to it. It's so hard to move here."

"I get it. I scuba dive a lot and love the way the water holds you up."

"Yes, it seems hard to balance on land," she said and steered around a family walking on the sand.

Marcus made sure she caught the intrigued glance he gave her. They made their way slowly back toward the strip of restaurants, the lights like fireflies in the dark.

"And how do you know English, er, this language?" Marcus was glad they could communicate but he had no idea how it was happening.

"We study as much of your culture as we can. Mermaids are capable of several languages."

"This is surreal." He grinned.

Marcus could tell she'd never had much male attention from the way she was blushing and uncomfortable. It made him feel like shit for stringing her along so easily but the cost could be lives.

"Hey, you want to go out for a ride on my boat?" he asked and was surprised when he felt excited at her complete agreement.

They walked toward the marina. Only a few clouds marred the bright sunlight and a breeze kicked up the ocean smell. They had reached the dock when a sharp voice called out.

"So you tell me to hide and you're out with another woman."

Marcus turned and faced a rightfully angry Jane. He closed his eyes briefly, searching for the courage to face his girlfriend. She was an awesome sight with her flaxen hair flying in the wind and blue eyes narrowed. Muriel was obviously confused by the other woman.

"Hey, Jane! This is my friend Muriel," he said, trying to play it casual and cool. "Could you give us a few minutes?" His eyes were apologetic.

Muriel merely nodded to them and walked away. Marcus saw her trying to remain calm and knew he'd hurt her.

Marcus spread his hands out in a gesture of surrender.

"Jane, this isn't what it looks like. You and I are in danger," he said earnestly. "I'm trying to buy my way out."

She cocked her hip, a feisty trait he both loved and hated about her. Jane pursed her lips.

"She looks like more than a friend, Marcus. And what danger am I in? I can help," she said resentfully.

"I need her for something. Can't you trust me?"

Jane rolled her eyes and tossed her silky hair. Hoop earrings dangled from her ears and shimmered in the moonlight. Marcus swallowed at what a beautiful woman he'd found. He didn't want to lose her.

"I trust you. What's this plan?" she asked determinedly.

Marcus could tell she wasn't going to leave. He made the only decision he could and took a deep breath.

# Chapter Twenty

Gabriel and Ephyra walked down a brightly lit Main Street. She was peering into every window, eyeing every car that passed. Even though he could handle the thought of her being royalty he wasn't sure he could handle falling for her anymore. She was a beacon of strength among women he'd dated. Her energy alone made him want to be more, go further.

"Do you think Jake's already learned to drive and stolen a car?" Gabriel teased.

She gave him a mock glare.

"I don't know. Jake is very resourceful."

Gabriel felt her little jolts every time he brushed her skin with his hand or arm. He liked the way it made her blush as she tried to ignore it. Ever since the cave she'd been different and he couldn't' say he disliked it.

"He has brown hair, brown eyes," she continued.

"So, we're searching for pretty much half the population," Gabriel joked.

He kept his eyes peeled nonetheless. Some part of him wondered if this Jake was someone he'd have problems with. He didn't want to presume to understand mermaid relationships but also knew he had found someone so rare that it would take a hell of a lot for him to let go.

He noted Ephyra's somber face and wished she would smile again. Gabriel kept making excuses to be closer to her as they walked. It seemed almost second nature to take her hand and she didn't protest. He felt awake; the kind of awake that a cold shower jolts you into.

For some reason, all the radios they passed were playing sappy love songs. Gabriel fell prey even more to the spell Ephyra was casting. He spied an exotic flower stand and while she was searching a café, he bought her a red and yellow hibiscus to put in her hair.

"Thank you," she said as he tucked the stem behind her ear and smoothed her hair over the spot.

He smiled and was rewarded by one in return. He knew it was stupid to carry this further but his heart refused to care. He loved that she was softer toward him, her eyes didn't hold that wariness anymore at him.

"What's wrong?" Ephyra asked in the intensity of his gaze.

"Nothing. You're just very beautiful," he said truthfully.

"Oh, that's very kind to say." Ephyra clearly wasn't sure what to do with a compliment.

Gabriel didn't want to make her uncomfortable with flattery so he pressed her for more information.

"There's so much I don't know, and I wish I had time to explore it," she said.

"Yea?" Gabriel smiled. "And what exactly is the rush?"

"It's complicated. I don't know if you'd believe me even if I told you," Ephyra said with a wry grin.

"You're probably right," Gabriel laughed.

"Do you believe in magic?" she asked.

"I believe that you're a mermaid," he said carefully.

Ephyra took a breath and then looked at him as if what she was about to say would make him run away.

"True. The magic I speak of is hidden in runes and ancient locks beneath the sea. A sea witch brought me here to hide from a merlord who has risen from his imprisonment and he wants to take over the realms of the sea."

Gabriel wasn't sure whether he wanted to fight her on this or just believe. He'd never actually seen her change into a human, of course—for that matter, he had no proof she'd ever sported a tail—but her explanation did make sense in a freakishly fantastical way.

"Is this why Jake is so important?"

"Yes, he protects me."

Gabriel felt there was more she wanted to say but she bit her lip worriedly.

"Tell you what, let's forget about merlords and war for tonight. We have a fun human custom I'd like to show you," he said and stood, holding out his hand.

Ephyra smiled up at him as he extended his hand. Gabriel didn't let go of it as they walked out into humid, cool air. Lights sparkled off the many clubs and onto the water like fireflies.

"Where are we going?" she asked playfully."You'll see."

They stopped at a building bursting with lights and music. Palm trees gracefully framed the entrance and wait staff dressed in white suit coats rushed around with food on trays.

"Will you be dining tonight?" a man asked politely.

"We'd like a couple of drinks. Is the dance floor open?" Gabriel asked with a smile.

The man grinned and nodded. "This way."

"I thought we could dance," Gabriel told her as they sat at a table covered in white linen.

"I don't know how."

"I don't know either. It's not hard, we just sway together." Gabriel joked.

A waiter arrived to take their order. Gabriel ordered lemon chicken and Ephyra ended up with the pasta.

"I've never had lettuce," she said with a raised brow, when the waiter had gone, announcing he'd bring their salads out.

"It's like seaweed except I think it'll taste better." Gabriel smiled and held out his hand. "Dance?"

Gabriel felt her uncertainty but held her firmly and she was soon swaying in time with him. He liked the feel of her skin and the way she had to tilt her head up to look at him.

"Am I doing dancing correctly?" she asked breathlessly.

"Yes," he responded, his breath close to her ear.

Gabriel wondered if she'd be alarmed if he kissed her again. Ephyra swayed toward him and Gabriel got his answer. He bent down and touched his lips to hers. Heat flashed between them and Gabriel felt her opening her mouth to his.

Gabriel distantly heard his cell ringing but he ignored it. He chose to massage Ephyra's lips with his and lose himself in her. It was almost painful how much he wanted her.

"I think your box is ringing," Ephyra said, breaking their kiss.

"I hate cell phones." He answered it curtly, moving to sit back down at the table.

His brother's annoying voice was on the other end, asking for Ephyra.

"Apparently, Muriel wants to speak with you," he said and handed it to Ephyra.

The mermaid accepted it gingerly and put it to her ear like she'd seen Gabriel do. He broke into a grin and pushed it closer to her ear.

"Muriel?" she shouted.

"You don't have to yell," he whispered. Ephyra gave him a smile and nodded.

"Muriel, can you hear me?" she said speaking normally.

Gabriel listened with half an ear to the entire conversation since Muriel obviously didn't get the memo that she didn't have to shout into the phone. He heard the other mermaid's distress.

"I want to show Marcus my other form tonight. I have the moonstone and I think I'll be okay if I show him . . . "

"You know the consequences, Muriel," Ephyra said authoritatively but sad.

Gabriel watched her blink away tears before handing him the phone. He hung it up.

"You all right?"

"Can we go to the bay tonight? Muriel wants to show your brother her true form."

"You don't sound like this is a good idea." He was getting a strange vibe from her.

"A mermaid loses her powers when she shows a human her true form but it sounds important to Muriel for some reason."

"I'm going to call him," Gabriel said darkly.

"No, she wants to show him and it's her choice."

"He doesn't know; if I tell him I can stop him from doing this."

"I won't take that choice away from her," Ephyra said fiercely.

Gabriel felt as if his head was overloaded with information. He was fuming that Marcus was going through with a dumb plan but there was no way he'd let Muriel be alone.

## Chapter Twenty-One

The night air was ripe with moisture but an east breeze swept in off the water. The bay was deserted and they could see the lights from the city glistening on the surface of the waves.

Marcus felt a current of electricity running through the water as he stepped into it. He nervously had a camera in his pocket and watched as Ephyra went to her friend. He could feel her tension and was sure she would try to talk to him. But she didn't.

"Are you sure about this?" she asked her friend gently.

Muriel's eyes glittered strangely in the moonlight but she nodded.

"I do." She looked toward Marcus wistfully. "He's the only one I'd want to do this for. I can't explain it but I know I'll never get another chance."

Ephyra sighed but hugged her. She stepped back a little, the water barely touching her toes.

"It's your decision," she said and glanced at Marcus. He was transfixed on Muriel.

Muriel removed her light cotton dress, followed by the necklace and handed both to Ephyra. She knelt gracefully in the sand, the waves splashing up over her shoulders. There was a faint glow that started from her head and traveled down her body. Swiftly and smoothly like shedding skin, the transformation began.

Her legs fused into one large fin, split into two at the ends. Scales of yellow, green, and blue cascaded up and down Muriel's body, climbing as high as her breasts, but barely covering them. She lay on the ground and propped herself up on forearms. The glow died around her but the moonlight took its place, showering her with translucent light.

Marcus felt his jaw drop and he struggled not to pinch himself.

He numbly had the camera out and was snapping pictures without even looking through the view finder. She hadn't been lying—Muriel just melted into a mermaid.

The thought shocked him more than he'd thought it would. She didn't look like a human in a mermaid suit; her fins weren't jointed where a human's legs and ankles would be. Her tail was gorgeous, complete muscle and smoothly covered in interlocking scales. He knelt down next to her, not touching but wanting to know she was real. Marcus could feel the heat emanating from her, the tickle of her hair as it blew in the wind.

Muriel bent her head and he tentatively reached out to tilt her chin to meet his gaze. He smiled gently at her. The guilt had fled to the back of his mind. He only felt awe and passion toward this beautiful creature.

"You're gorgeous," he whispered.

Muriel smiled shyly. She let him lean closer and brush her tail. She shivered, but allowed him to feel the smooth scales, each part of an ornate pattern on her tail.

Marcus marveled at the warmth of her body. He couldn't breathe at this wonderful creature's surrender to him. She lay still but relaxed. All at once, his plan shattered. Marcus felt tears in his eyes. I'm a son of a bitch, he thought bitterly. He glanced involuntarily toward the dark shadows, wondering if Sanchez was there, where he'd told him to be.

"Muriel," Marcus started but the words stuck in his throat. How could he tell her he'd sold her secret? He shook his head, tears falling down his cheeks.

With the last of his courage, he closed his eyes, touched her chin gently and closed his lips over hers. He felt her stiffen in surprise and then almost desperately kiss him back.

Marcus broke apart first and peered into her eyes, seeing the way she saw him. It filled him with shame.

"Get out of here," he cried and stood abruptly.

Marcus hauled Muriel out of the water and tried to get her to land but her fins were cumbersome. He put the necklace back on, but nothing happened. Her sad eyes were like accusations piercing his heart.

"It won't work on me again. I can't change because I've revealed myself to you." Muriel's face crumbled as she glanced past Ephyra. Tears flowed down her petite face, making her eyes look like fallen stars.

Muriel placed the stone back in Ephyra's hand.

"We have to get you out of here." Out of the corner of his eye, Marcus saw Sanchez and his men were running down to them. He shoved Muriel back into the waves and fell with her. Her tail flashed in the moonlight and the surf covered them both.

"Muriel!" Marcus's scream tore the air.

He saw men grab for her but instead they got Ephyra instead. Marcus plunged toward them but felt men grabbing his arms and twisting them. Someone pulled his camera from his pocket and he hoped it was wet enough to be ruined now.

"Hey!" Gabriel's shout rent the air like a shot. Marcus saw his brother running at the tangle of confusion.

He watched Gabriel desperately throwing punches and landing kicks. The other men were better and Marcus punched the nearest one that dunked Gabe's head under the water. The guy let him up but Marcus felt his nose explode in pain.

Then, almost as quickly as they'd come they left. Sanchez whistled and they all piled into their black cars. Ephyra disappeared with them and Muriel was long gone under the water.

Gabriel lowered his hands and faced his brother, a furious glare on his face. Marcus shielded his face for a moment, certain a punch was coming his way. When none did, he dared to lower them and saw the pain on Gabriel's face.

"This was the plan?" Gabriel's voice was low and deadly calm.

"I'm sorry." It was all he could say and he knew it wasn't adequate. "I never meant to . . . " Marcus sighed. The truth was he had meant for Sanchez to go home with a mermaid—just not Ephyra.

"What the fuck are we supposed to do now?" Gabriel roared,

his anger finally overwhelming his sense of control. Marcus wisely backed away a few steps but wouldn't have defended himself if Gabriel started raining more punches at his head. Marcus felt blood drying on his face.

"Perhaps I can be of service, since you two morons have done a great job so far," a new voice piped up.

Gabriel and Marcus turned as a unit to see a broad shouldered man, with dark hair and eyes that seemed to have a predatory amber glow. At least he was clothed.

"Let me guess, you're a mermaid, too. Jake?" Gabriel sighed and gave him a tight smile.

"Merman, actually." The human man said with a swaggering frown.

# Chapter Twenty-Two

Ephyra was taken into a corridor lined with doors in a dark, Spartan building. She felt the ties around her hands loosen and she pulled her sore arms in front of her.

"Don't try anything," the man next to her warned.

She didn't intend to until she'd observed possible routes of escape. Ephyra was led into a large room with an illuminated tank of water that encompassed the entire wall. She had an ominous feeling as they made her sit next to it. The tank hummed with some sort of machinery and she saw bubbles rising in the pristine water.

"What now?" The man asked into his phone.

He nodded and motioned to the other men. They each took one of Ephyra's arms and the man in the middle started to unbutton her shorts.

"Hey!" she protested but the men held her tight.

Within minutes, her clothes had been tugged or cut off her. Ephyra saw her shorts tossed away, the necklace still safe in the pocket. She stood naked and unashamed. Ephyra knew human women preferred to never be seen unclothed by strangers. She didn't care. Her body may not have been perfect but by their hungry stares, the men were aroused.

"What was that for?" she asked bitterly. Perhaps it had been the short time with Gabriel but she found she didn't want anyone else seeing her like this but him.

They didn't answer but just waited, staring at her. Their eyes traced every curve and lingered over her breasts and the V between her legs. Ephyra shook her head in disgust. As long as they didn't touch her she could keep her wits. She used the time to get her bearings, noting the room had a single door, mirrors on the wall and a mini bar to the right. The man named Sanchez strolled in through that only entry.

He smiled at her and even his eyes lingered on her nude form inappropriately. Ephyra could feel her skin crawling with repugnance.

"Our own little mermaid," he said with an amused smile. "I'd very much like to see you in your true form."

Ephyra frowned at him. For one thing, he didn't know the consequences he asked for and she was sure he wouldn't care if he did.

"I'm not a mermaid," she lied and for now it was true. She couldn't change back into her form at will.

"Liar. We saw you change, or is this a trick?" Sanchez narrowed his beady eyes. "Does Mr. Rayner think he can fool me?"

Ephyra realized he was talking of Marcus and not Gabriel. It almost gave her comfort to know Gabriel would come after her, yet at the same time she didn't want to put him in more danger.

"What will motivate you to change, my dear?" Sanchez said and motioned to his men.

They grabbed her and just as she feared, opened the top of the tank. Ephyra struggled but she found her human body lacking. It was strong but not against three men who were all a head taller and outweighed her by at least seventy pounds. She plunged into the tank and the water made her gasp as it streamed into her mouth and nose.

"I'm not a mermaid!" she shouted, hoping they could hear her through the glass.

The men latched the lid and stood back. Ephyra had inches to breath and she tilted her head up to suck in oxygen. She was furious but no amount of pounding would break the glass. The water was all wrong anyway as she tasted it. The salinity content was off; no fish could even live in it.

Ephyra watched as Sanchez opened a small hole at the top and poured more water in. Her eyes widened in fear as the water level rose. Soon she was completely submerged and for once Ephyra felt the terrifying grip of not being able to breathe under water. She felt a tingling in her chest that soon was giving rise to panic. There was no air!

She struggled to remain conscious but lack of oxygen was making her vision fuzzy. Her lungs burned for release but none came. Ephyra sank to the bottom of the tank, passing into unconsciousness.

Sanchez waited a moment before he cursed angrily.

"Lower the water, get her up, now," he commanded. The men used a long pool stick to lift her up to the surface and began to lift her out.

"Does she need CPR?" Sanchez asked, wanting her alive. Perhaps the mermaid needed something different to change.

"She's coming around, she was only under a minute."

Ephyra coughed and sputtered, her lungs heaving in air. She opened her eyes but before she could regain control of her limbs, she felt herself pushed back into the water. Ephyra desperately grabbed for the side of the edge but they pried her fingers off. The lid shut as she gained consciousness and she could stand on tiptoe to breathe at the surface. Ephyra gasped for a few minutes and her heart rate began to slow from its race with death.

She looked out to see Sanchez conferring with his men. He turned to her with a sadistic stare.

"What do you need to change, mermaid? You'd best tell me or it will be a long life for you in a tank," he sneered.

"I'm . . . not a mermaid." She stuck to her lie weakly.

She almost wished she could change to never experience drowning again. The utter lonely darkness and choking was more terrifying than she'd imagined. All the old stories of mermaids pulling sailors to their deaths made her appreciate the fact that merfolk were forbidden to do this now. She couldn't imagine what their last moments were as oxygen ran out and the lungs felt as if they'd burst.

"Perhaps some more incentive." Sanchez whirled on his heel and strode purposefully out the door.

Ephyra let her head rest against the glass. She had always thought humans keeping fish in a glass tank was their way of appreciating the ocean's life. Now, she wanted to smash every glass box. The room went dark except for the lights around the bar and in her tank. Both gave off an electric blue glow.

# Chapter Twenty-Three

Gabriel stared almost resentfully at this merman parading as a human. Jake gave him a level stare back. He had curling brown hair that seemed to change shades in different light, the same went for his eyes. They weren't a plain brown but golden with flecks of green. Gabriel slapped himself mentally. What was he doing, gazing like a chick into Jake's eyes? He shook his head angrily.

"So, you're the one Ephyra is looking for," Marcus said in the growing silence.

Gabriel didn't bother to glance at him. He knew Marcus wanted to make amends desperately. There was no use making him grovel.

"I asked to be sent wherever she was to help her," Jake said with a maddeningly polite smile at him.

Gabriel ground his teeth.

"So, when I get her back you're just going to take her away again?" Gabriel asked, crossing his arms over his chest. He knew Jake didn't miss his use of "I."

"She'll come whether she wants to or not. There's a war going on under the ocean, boys. Something I gather she hasn't told you," Jake said pointedly.

Gabriel was forced to concede round one to him. Ephyra hadn't elaborated on the warlord she'd mentioned. He thought back and remembered how agitated she'd been to get away from him. He'd held her up, distracting her. Trying to romance a woman who wasn't really a woman, no, a princess who wasn't human.

"You seem oddly well adjusted."

"I have human contacts that the merfolk don't know about. It's a gift."

"What's your plan, then, playboy?" Gabriel spat. "Do you

mermen have laser vision, super powers, or some other more conceivable way to find Ephyra?"

His sarcasm apparently was not lost on Jake.

"You have a very bad temper," Jake scolded. "As it so happens, I did not come unprepared. I have stored weapons on a boat I procured, from above mentioned contacts."

"Weapons?" Marcus said hopefully.

"You mean pieces of coral and sea shells?"

Gabriel saw the merman finally give way to anger. For a moment Gabriel thought he was going to throw a punch. He wondered if the merman was even happy being in human form.

"You two fools are on your own then if you don't want my help," Jake said finally.

Gabriel weighed the options carefully. The merman probably needed their help as much as they needed his. Gabriel saw the same concern and love for Ephyra mirrored in Jake's eyes. He suddenly understood something clearer.

"Wait."

Jake sighed but turned to look at Gabriel.

"How long have you known Ephyra?" He saw Jake sag slightly. It was the weight of a man haunted.

"I grew up with her," he confessed proudly.

Gabriel heard the desire in his voice, the swiftness with which he would lay down his life for her. He knew the feeling only recently, but it was consuming him like a beautiful virus. They were in love with the same woman.

"Then we have the same goal," he said evenly. "I think we need to work together."

Jake nodded slowly. "I can afford to be cooperative right now or I wouldn't have come to you."

"Marcus, you can't come with us—they know you too well. Jake, we need to get to your boat and see these weapons," Gabriel instructed.

"They've seen you, too, Gabe," Marcus pointed out.

"I don't care. Better get your boat, or Jake's, ready. We need to relocate." Gabriel thought about where they could go.

"Tortola," Marcus suggested. "The British Virgin Islands are close and I have a friend there."

"A friend?" Gabriel raised a brow skeptically.

"She's said to be a witch doctor so no one bothers her. I met her through unscrupulous means, sure, but I helped her," Marcus said evasively.

"Okay, Tortola," Gabriel agreed. "Do you have any idea where Ephyra would be?" Gabriel asked his brother. Marcus shook his head.

"I do," Jake said unexpectedly and strode out the door assuming they'd follow. He paused. "Actually, pack up and check out of this hotel. You won't be coming back."

In twenty minutes, Gabriel loaded his suitcases in the rental car and had checked out of the Marquesa. He looked over at Jake who sat in the front seat, marveling at the seat belt.

"Hey, McGyver, what's next?" Gabriel said and ripped the shiny buckle from Jake's hands.

"Who?" Jake asked and picked up the buckle again. "We could really use these contraptions on dolphins and swordfish."

Gabriel rolled his eyes.

"Never mind."

"So, follow the trail of slime," Jake said and muttered some foreign words.

Gabriel saw a glowing green trail of slime appear as they pulled into the area near the bay. His heart contracted as he left the beach where Ephyra had been a mere hour ago.

"It's a hyacinth snail. I put them on all the cars, yours too, because I wasn't sure who I should be tailing," Jake explained.

"Oh." Gabriel shrugged. It was good thinking. "How long will this trail last? We don't have any weapons or a plan here."

"It'll last for as long as I'm alive or until I erase it. But if we wait too long they could move her. I can't put snails on living beings."The moonlight was enough they could see *Revenge* on the backside of the boat Jake had purchased as they pulled into the parking lot next to the dock. Gabriel instantly liked the sixty-foot sailboat. She didn't look particularly posh but she was big enough to sail them and their equipment to Tortola.

"Here they are," Jake said as they climbed aboard and ducked into the pit.

Gabriel's eyes widened in surprise at the arsenal. Guns, knives, and some weapons he didn't even recognize draped the table and couches.

"Are those AK47s?" Gabriel asked in awe. He wasn't sure on the surface if he could shoot a person, but then he hadn't been in love with the target.

"I don't know, are they?" Jake shrugged. "I'm not quite sure about all your weapons."

"That would be an M16, too."

"You have a military grade gun here?" Marcus asked nervously. "Who did you get these from?"

"A contact," Jake said with a wink.

"I hope you know what you're doing," Marcus answered.

"If I fail Ephyra and she fails, then the world is doomed anyway," Jake responded cryptically.

"Excuse me?" Gabriel paused in loading practicing a shotgun. "World doom?"

"Ephyra didn't tell you much, huh?" Jake guessed. "There is a leader of the underworld, Erebos, who controls a dark race of merfolk that have been gathering for years. They finally have enough in numbers and now even your realm is in danger."

"How can land be danger if he's bound under water?" Gabriel asked, his head spinning with the mythical twist his life had taken.

"He will drown all land until the oceans cover it," Jake said flatly. "Last I checked, humans can't breathe under water."

Marcus started to load the AK.

The situation was almost comical enough to make Gabriel

chuckle. He had done nothing more exciting than suspending one of his students and now there was talk of warlords, mermaids, and the end of the world.

"What's the hilarity?" Jake asked, confused at the smile Gabriel couldn't suppress.

"Nothing. Let's just get out of here and come up with a plan," Gabriel said, still grinning.

Gabriel picked up a Kevlar vest to wear under his shirt, feeling like he was dressing up for Halloween, and loaded extra clips into the pockets. He tossed more ammunition and the M16s in a black bag. Jake watched him with a puzzled but curious expression.

"You don't know how to use these, do you?" It wasn't accusatory, just a statement.

Jake shook his head.

"I am afraid I didn't study your weapons as well as I should have. I have my own set here but I'm not sure how well they will work on humans," he motioned to a set of gold knives and a ram's horn device.

"This will take longer than I thought." Gabriel ran a hand through his hair. It was growing out and the distant thought crossed his mind he'd need it cut soon.

He picked up the 9mm and slanted it sideways to show it to Jake. "This has 9 millimeter bullets, fairly small but they'll do significant damage to any human. Any fish really," he snorted. "Trigger, safety, sights."

Gabriel demonstrated how to sight the pistol, load the clip, and put it in the gun. It was a good review for him since it'd been a while since his hunting days with his father. Marcus interjected a few tips of his own, having owned a variety of guns his entire life.

"Are mermen immortal?" Marcus asked as the gun lesson ended.

Jake smiled wryly.

"If we were, would I have brought weapons of both my kind and yours?" He tilted his head at them as if they were stupid.

Gabriel laughed. They deserved it.

"Now, tell me if you want to use my weapons?" Jake asked and picked up the ram's horn. He pushed a hidden trigger on the side in one of the circles and the horn started to glow a light red color.

"Whoa," Marcus eyed the horn with interest.

"What does it do?" Gabriel asked. He glimpsed a barrel-like structure at the end of the horn.

"I can't use it now, but it shoots poisonous urchin spikes." Jake pressed the trigger again and the horn stopped glowing.

"I'm not exactly a John Wayne with a pistol, so let's take that, too," Gabriel said with a nod.

Jake seemed pleased and started to pack his equipment. They left Marcus to man the boat, ready to take them to the island. Marcus would leave his own boat so it wouldn't be recognized.

"Good luck," Marcus said in parting, and Gabriel smiled tightly. He wished they'd had time to practice with the weapons, but he'd rescue Ephyra no matter how bad of a marksmen he was.

*

The trail of green slime led them twisting down streets full of partiers, tourists and night life. After what seemed an interminable amount of time, the trail ended at two black BMWs sitting on the side of an alley warehouses on either side. One looked like a club and the other abandoned.

"Pick your poison," Gabriel said to Jake. He grudgingly admitted Jake's snail trick was a good one.

"Left one," Jake said and they slipped from the car toward the darker building. No movement anywhere made Gabriel nervous. The shadows seemed to reach out as they sidled up to the building from the right.

Jake motioned to the nearest door. Gabriel nodded, pulled his Glock and pressed against the door. He listened for any movement inside. Only silence met his straining ears. Gabriel tried the handle gently, not surprised to find it locked. He shook his head at Jake, who stood a few paces away.

They made their way around the building, checking doors and peeking in windows. The warehouse was tightly sealed all around. Gabriel was starting to think they should just check the other building when Jake pulled out four round devices. He handed two to Gabriel, who almost recoiled at the cold sliminess.

"What is this?" he whispered.

"Squid hooks, watch." Jake placed the suction cup on each hand and it melded into his palm. He grinned at Gabriel and then placed his hands on the brick wall. Slowly, he ascended using his arms.

"Race you to the top," Jake called down.

Gabriel's lips curved into a competitive smile. He squished the squid hooks on his palms and crawled up the wall, putting him even with Jake. Once over the roof railing, Gabriel found himself standing with a spectacular view of the city lights spotlighting the city like beacons against the ocean churning like a monster in the dark, waiting.

Gabriel spied the emergency doors. He walked gingerly toward them, unsure how much sound could be heard on the roof. He tried the doors, betting they'd be locked.

"Do you have anything else?" Gabriel whispered.

Jake placed his hands on the door, squid hooks still on his palms. He shrugged as he tried to pull the door open. The hooks stretched and strained until Gabriel thought they'd break. All at once, the door handle popped off and the door cracked slightly. Gabriel nodded, impressed. He placed his own suctioned hand on the door and pulled it all the way open.

They stared into a dark hall with stairs leading down. It was the only direction they had so both men followed it. Dimly lit emergency exits glowed overhead. The building was clearly not as abandoned as it appeared. They could hear music pumping not just from the club but from within the building they were in.

Gabriel stepped lightly down the stairs, sweat beginning to bead on his forehead and down his neck. The humidity was stifling in the stairwells. He noticed with annoyance Jake didn't appear to be perspiring.

"This is going to take too long," he whispered to Gabriel as they reached the third floor.

"Split up?" Gabriel suggested. He wasn't particularly keen on this but they needed to cover as much ground as possible. Who knew what Sanchez was doing to Ephyra in the hours he'd had her already? A strange pulse beat in his head as he thought of what he'd do to anyone who'd touched her.

"I'll look around here, you go down," Jake said and strode confidently down the hallway out of sight.

Gabriel made his way down to the next floor.

# Chapter Twenty-Four

Ephyra's legs were getting tired of supporting her in the tank. She felt her skin wrinkling and it was disgusting her. Her body was stretched out for all to see and she had given up glaring at every man who stood watching her with their eyes glazed over.

Sanchez suddenly appeared and she was alert.

The lid was opened so she could hear and Ephyra watched as he dragged in a man with a hood over his head. The man was forced to kneel, his hands bound behind his back. She shifted in the water restlessly, afraid of what Sanchez wanted to do to this man.

"This man is innocent, mermaid. Don't your people like that kind of man?" Sanchez said with a snicker. "If I give him to you will you change?"

Ephyra curled her lip. This was what he thought she needed? A human man? She thought of Gabriel, his safe, warm embrace.

"Do you not speak anymore?" Sanchez yelled. He pulled out his shiny silver 9mm and pointed it at the man's leg.

Ephyra had never been near a gun but she knew they were dangerous. The shot blasted her ears and the man's screams pulled at her heart. She saw blood spray from his shattered thigh and the man fell over, thrashing in agony.

"Isn't it legend that mermaids can save dying men? He'll bleed out soon," Sanchez shouted at her, waving the gun.

Ephyra felt tears welling in her eyes. This man would die because she was unable to save him. The sea witch had taken all her powers when she'd turned human.

"I can't help him!" she cried and pounded on the glass.

Sanchez had two of his men uncover the man's head and, heaving, they shoved him into the tank. Ephyra moved out of the way just in time as the man's body crashed into the water. It instantly turned pink with his blood. She dove to help him to the surface but saw he wasn't conscious anymore. He was young, a tanned face with curly blond hair.

She fumbled with the ties around his hands but they wouldn't give. Ephyra gave up and simply propped his head up above the water. He breathed shallowly.

Sanchez watched Ephyra try to save the man but she still did not change. He turned to his head man, James.

"You did grab the mermaid, chico?" he asked condescendingly.

The man visibly swallowed.

"I am pretty sure, sir, but we should have waited until they were out of the water . . . " his voice died at Sanchez's glare.

"We?"

"I should have waited to give the signal." James bowed his head.

"So, you're saying there is a possibility this woman is just a human?" Sanchez glanced at Ephyra trying to hold the dead man.

"I don't know, sir. There were a lot of unexpected people there," James said, cringing.

"Have you found Marcus yet?"

"We're searching. Marcus hasn't been back to his house," James responded.

"And his girlfriend?"

"She is in hiding. But we'll find her."

Sanchez instructed two of his men to pull Ephyra out. She was too exhausted to fight as she was plucked from the tank. They left the man, who sank to the bottom of the tank.

"He's still alive!" she shouted and struggled against the men. They seemed to enjoy it as their hands brushed her body.

"I don't see him breathing," Sanchez said coldly.

"Why do you do this?" Ephyra sobbed angrily. She twisted to see the man bleeding out in the water, his head sagging, his eyes still closed.

"Do you know what expendable means?" Sanchez asked.

There was a deafening blast and Ephyra saw the tank explode, water gushing out and the dead man sliding out to knock into the circle around her. She leapt up and tried to pry their hands off her.

In a dark blur she saw Gabriel's familiar form tackling the man closest to her. His punches came fast and sharp and he used the gun in his hand to hammer at heads. Ephyra backed away as the men's attention shifted from her to him. She dove for her shorts and was relieved to find the necklace still in the pocket.

Bloodied noses, scratched faces and bruised eyes surrounded Gabriel. Gabriel finally backed up, aiming to grab the black bag he'd dropped.He kicked out quickly with his left leg and the man went down with a grunt. He dove for the bag but another saw what he was going after and pulled his gun. Gabriel pulled his own gun and they stood at a standstill. He grabbed the downed man and pointed it to his head.

"Don't move," Gabriel said, breathing hard. A trickle of blood ran down his face.

The man stared him down until a spike shot through his chest. He stared down at it for a moment and then fell forward. Gabriel smiled as Jake stood in the doorway, the ram's horn glowing and primed. Ephyra gasped in relief at seeing her friend.

"I think I just saved your life," Jake said with a grin and then aimed the horn.

Before Ephyra could scream out a warning, Gabriel raised his own weapon toward a shadow behind Jake. He squeezed the trigger and the bullet exploded into the shadow that fell back.

"And we're even," he said and put in a new clip.

"Ephyra," Jake said, his gaze suddenly distracted.

Ephyra looked at her two rescuers and her eyes filled with tears. She stepped forward, not knowing who she wanted to hug first. Gabriel stepped in front of Jake.

"Why do I always seem to find you naked?" he teased gently.

Ephyra laughed tearfully and ran to him, falling into his strong arms. She felt him squeeze her hard, his breath rushing out in a relieved sigh. Ephyra was mildly annoyed she needed anyone to save her but somehow, because it was Gabriel, it was right.

She finally drew back and her eyes lighted on Jake. Ephyra smiled widely at her friend and at the merfolk weapon in his hand. She knew he'd come prepared.

"Jake!" Ephyra cried happily.

Jake instantly tried to bow like a merman and then just fell to one knee, head down. Ephyra frowned at his formality. Their friendship wasn't bound by royal threat. She gently lifted his face and his golden eyes looked up into hers. She saw them filled with a pain that she'd never seen before.

"Why do you not embrace me as a friend?"

Jake let out a long sigh but his mouth curved into a smile. He stood and put a hand on her shoulder.

"I am very glad to have found you," he said simply.

Ephyra was stung. She pulled back crossly. What was the matter with him? She noticed Gabriel wasn't as puzzled.

"Thank you for your rescue, Jahayl," Ephyra addressed him coldly with his formal mername. Jake nodded and led the way out of the building.

*

Ephyra slipped into the passenger seat of Gabriel's car, and Jake hopped into the back seat.

"Do they know you're a mermaid?" Gabriel asked her as they drove toward the dock.

"No. They tried to drown me but I couldn't change even then," Ephyra said quietly.

"What?" Both men shouted. Gabriel's grip on the wheel tightened angrily.

"I didn't have Muriel's necklace."

Ephyra made eye contact with Jake in the back seat. From his expression she knew he'd seen Muriel reveal herself.

"I should have stopped this," Gabriel was saying.

"It's no one's fault, she chose to do it."

"If you call stripping her of dignity and power, sure," Jake interjected.

"I didn't know the severity." Gabriel met his gaze in the rearview mirror.

"I didn't tell you," Ephyra sighed and wished she were alone with Gabriel to explain.

Gabriel excused himself as they pulled into Marcus' dock and Ephyra turned accusingly to her friend with blazing eyes.

"What's the matter with you?"

"I'm fine, Ephyra. Just glad I was able to find you in time. Did they hurt you?" he asked, amber eyes flashing.

"They tried." Ephyra frowned at him. Why was he being so distant?

"So, you think Muriel did a foolish thing for love?" she asked him quietly.

The answer was in his eyes. They avoided her gaze and were tinged with such sadness that she reached out to touch his shoulder.

Jake jolted as if she'd electrocuted him. He let her hand linger for a moment but then shrugged it off.

"I think love is a very powerful tool that we all use differently."

"Thank you for coming for me," she said softly, afraid she knew why he was behaving this way.

Jake finally reached up to cup her face in his large hand. Ephyra sighed in relief and leaned into his warm palm.

"You can't believe that I wouldn't have," he whispered. Ephyra shook her head and took his hand.

"I can't love you the way you love me," she said saw his eyes close as if in pain.

"I know." Jake dropped his hand from hers and sat back in the seat. He seemed resigned to leave it at that and Ephyra felt too much emotion to say more.

Gabriel returned to the car with a worried expression.

"I can't find Marcus anywhere on board," he said opening the car door and sitting in the driver's seat. Ephyra was glad he seemed not to notice the tension.

"Do you think Sanchez found him?" Jake asked.

"There weren't any signs of struggle and the weapons are still there," Gabriel said worriedly.

"He'll show up then—he's alive. Are you suggesting we wait for him?" Jake asked pointedly. They didn't have a lot of time and Sanchez had probably already found his men dead and the tank busted.

"I don't know." Gabriel's blue eyes were clouded with anxiety. Ephyra touched his elbow and gave him a reassuring smile.

"He'll turn up. I'm afraid I've put you and Marcus in too much danger already," she said quietly.

Gabriel swung to face her, his facc carnest.

"No you haven't. I shouldn't even care about him right now. It's his fault we're in this mess!" Gabriel struggled to control his temper. "I guess we'll sleep the night on the boat and wait until tomorrow. I'll move it a few moorings down, just in case he brings more trouble with him."

Ephyra felt her insides doing a strange dance at his confidence and protectiveness. She'd been protected her entire life but this was something new. Gabriel wasn't under any obligation to do it and yet he protected her more fiercely than any guard had. She was afraid of the dependency she was forming with him but at the same time she couldn't imagine being without him.

They hunkered down in the boat, parking the car at a distance in case someone had seen and marked it. Ephyra offered Jake the couch but he chose to remain topside. She let Gabriel lead her into the cabin and make up the fold-out bed. He turned on a fan and the breeze helped move the humid, stale air. Ephyra lay down and was comforted with his bulk next to her. The soft washing of the waves and rocking of the boat put her into a deep sleep.

## Chapter Twenty-Five

Scyllane's whole body felt like it had been eaten by an orca and vomited out. Her tail hurt to move courtesy of Sevag's impromptu surgery. Hate welled up in her so strong she shook with it. She remained chained to the piece of rock but was given room to lay down now.

She didn't know what day it was, but her internal clock estimated it was nearly dawn. This far down the sunlight did not penetrate the water and it remained the same shade of gloom all the time.

"From a fallen place she will seek, on burnished heels to spring from light, his soul on fire to the darkness he shall meet, a slave for the eternal fight," she chanted the ancient prophecy to herself.

She prayed for the words to get to Ephyra's ears. She'd studied a long time to learn how to read the ocean's history and runes on the stones. She saw her mirror slowly come to her side as if summoned. The currents must have picked it up. Scyllane felt like it was her only friend at that moment and held her arms out for it. The gilded handheld mirror softly landed in her palms as she looked into its reflective surface.

She saw the welts on her face and her scraggly her hair. Scyllane remembered a time when she'd had servants brush it twice a day, when rouge from lichens and blossom bottoms were applied to her lips and eyes. She decided she liked herself this way instead. She was real this way; her bruises had made her stronger.

Scyllane wished to see if Ephyra found her champion yet. The mirror glowed, its green surface blank for a moment but then images appeared. Scyllane gasped in surprise. The mirror showed Ephyra laying with a man, a human man with tousled dark sandy colored hair; his eyes were closed as he slept next to the mermaid.

Was this some sorcerer on land? Why could she see Ephyra

now? Scyllane didn't think he looked powerful, despite the muscle that bulged on his arms wrapped protectively around Ephyra. How had this human managed to hide her image from the mirror for so long? Scyllane felt a small smile light her face. Perhaps Ephyra had found something after all.

Scyllane felt the mirror change, the image stopped and the handle elongated into a fine point like short spear. She cocked her head and saw it aimed itself at the locks on the chains. Scyllane smiled at her friend and put the point in the key hole.

# Chapter Twenty-Six

Ephyra woke with a start. She heard the gentle slap of waves and felt her body rocking. She remembered they were on a boat and turned to see Gabriel slowly opening his eyes. They were startling blue up close, framed by dark lashes, and were directed at her. She smiled slightly.

He checked his watch. It was nearly eleven in the morning. They'd gotten about five hours of sleep and he was satisfied with that.

"I don't really sleep that much in the sea," she said with laugh. Ephyra rolled over to face him and touched his face tentatively. His jaw was rough with stubble and felt scratchy on her hand.

"I should find a razor," he said but made no move to sit up.

Ephyra saw desire, hard and electric go through his body, and it thrilled her. She'd never seen a man respond quite so quickly to her. Perhaps one . . . she thought of Jake up above. She felt stupid for not realizing sooner how Jake had felt about her.

"You'll be safe," Gabriel said, mistaking her apprehension for fear.

She just smiled at him and lay back, all thoughts of Jake disappearing. Ephyra was glad he followed her down, his mouth just inches away from hers. She felt a flush starting in her abdomen and radiating up to her cheeks. The light sheet they shared seemed constricting and she wanted it off. Gabriel shoved it from between them and suddenly she felt his leg on hers, his broad chest looming over her.

Ephyra waited, holding her breath. She wondered if all human women woke this way with their mates. Gabriel slowly lowered his head and touched her lips. She sighed in pleasure and let him caress her. Foreign warmth began to moisten between her legs and her breasts heaved to touch his bare chest. She found she wanted more than kisses now. Something made her grab his arms and tug him lower.

He slipped one hand down her slim neck, caressed her collar bone and then cupped her breast in his hand. Ephyra gasped at the unexpected pleasure and opened her eyes. It was nothing compared to what she'd read about when humans mated. She felt his fingers pinching her nipple through the shirt's fabric. All of the sudden she wanted that removed from between them, too.

As if reading her mind, Gabriel tugged the shirt off her shoulders baring her rosy nipples. He bent his head and lavished one with his tongue. Ephyra arched her neck back and unconsciously grabbed his hair, begging him to take it farther into his mouth.

"Oh . . . " she gasped as he moved to her other breast and suckled gently.

Gabriel drew back with a fiendish grin. He shifted position so his thigh pressed up between her legs. Then he took her finger and slipped it into his mouth, his tongue creating ecstasy.

Ephyra didn't have words for what she was feeling. There was no fear now, just a longing that had everything to do with him. She found the friction between her legs growing nearly unbearable as he moved slightly. Ephyra gazed between them, wondering if she was allowed to touch him.

"Tell me to stop anytime," Gabriel sighed and kissed her so deeply it left her breathless.

"Don't stop." She drew her finger out of his mouth and touched his bare chest, marveling at the lines and muscle. Her hands slid lower over his abdomen and then to the buckle at his pants. She hesitated and stared up at him, questioning. Gabriel just grinned at her and waited as she unzipped them.

She had seen anatomy pictures of human men, so his penis was no surprise. However, she didn't expect to be so turned on by it. If it was possible, the heat inside her grew. Ephyra lightly grazed his shaft with her fingertips and drew a moan from Gabriel. She drew back, afraid she'd caused him pain but saw he was writhing in pleasure instead. Ephyra smiled and touched it again. Gabriel shuddered at her touch.

Gabriel took her hands, pinned them above her head and suckled her breasts again, tasting each nipple, making her twist in the pleasure she'd trapped him in. She felt him caress her stomach down to her long legs and stop between them. With a smile, he dipped his head to lick her there.

Ephyra cried out at this new sensation. She writhed beneath him as his tongue did things to her that she never imagined. It was a human secret that she would never know as a mermaid. She closed her eyes and let herself fall into deeper circles of enjoyment.

Gabriel finally hovered over her, parting her legs as he looked into her eyes.

"I love you, Ephyra," he whispered fervently. "If it's too soon . . . hell, I'm apologizing. I love you." He strained to wait for her to open to him. Ephyra had never heard such sweet words.

"I love you, too." She had never uttered words that were so genuine. It didn't matter it had been only days since they'd met, she felt like she'd known him forever.

He gently pushed himself into her warmth. She gasped at the tightness, of how he filled her in a place she'd never known.

Ephyra felt a slight pain at first and struggled against him but as he let her get used to him, powerful sensations began to take hold of her body. She felt the boat rocking under them as Gabriel mimicked the motion. She was aware only of Gabriel's breathing, their hearts bursting with exertion. He plunged deeper inside her and she moaned at the feeling of his thickness, his intimacy. Ephyra thrust her hips forward instinctively, wanting him to go faster, harder. Gabriel complied and soon he was spiraling her into a frenzied high. They culminated in a clash of passion that left them both shaking.

Gabriel collapsed to the side of her, and she cuddled into him, relishing the scent of his sex and the sea.

"I do love you," she said sadly.

"Don't look at me like that." He smoothed some hair off her face.

"I can't be with you," Ephyra sighed sadly. "The war is coming.

You should know the truth."

Gabriel sat up and draped his shirt back over her in case someone came down. Ephyra wondered briefly if Jake knew what they'd done. She wasn't even quite sure herself except that she wanted to do it again. Soon.

"I'll do whatever you need. So, why can't you change into a mermaid?" he asked and listened attentively as she explained her family's massacre and the limited days she had left on land. Ephyra loved him all the more for trying to understand, especially the mercode for war and her search for a warrior.

"So, this sea witch made you human to hide you. Is she on your side or his?"

Ephyra shrugged and hoped Scyllane hadn't been killed by Erebos yet. She figured if she was still human, then the witch's spell was still intact. Still, Scyllane hadn't said if she perished the spell would revert.

"Erebos was supposed to be locked away for eternity," Ephyra said bitterly. "I'm only here because I have to find someone strong enough to fight . . . "

Gabriel frowned.

"We found Jake, are there more merpeople here?"

Ephyra smiled despite herself. Merpeople. She loved the way he used words.

"No, I have to find a warrior to fight for my realm. It's merfolk law that if the throne is challenged you have seven days to find a champion to face the opposing force's chosen champion. It was made so anyone could be a ruler, but my father banished it when it started a slave trade. Merfolk would start collecting the toughest merlings and train them to be warriors."

"Merlings?" Gabriel nipped at her lower lip despite the severity of what she was saying. Ephyra realized he thought she was cute.

"Babies. Merlings."

"Ah. So, you think there's a warrior on land that can fight in the water?" he asked skeptically.

She shrugged. "There must be."

"Is there any way you could just stay here?" He grasped at a long shot. She could tell he wanted to just pretend she wasn't what she said.

Ephyra could see the struggle on his face at the consequence of what they'd done. She was now irrevocably linked to him but her brain told her this wasn't possible.

"I don't know but I never thought I would love you this way," she said and rested her head on his chest. His breathing was soothing.

"I will help, Ephyra, I don't care what it takes." Despite the severity of his words, his stomach growled with hunger. She smiled up at him, feeling the first stirrings of hope. "I'll get food first and then we're going to think about all this quickly."

*

Fifteen minutes later, Gabriel's phone rang. It wasn't Marcus.

"Hey, Mom," he said with a grimace.

"Gabriel, how are you? Have you found Marcus? There's a big storm front coming to south Florida," his mother's chipper voice came over the line.

He could picture her alone in the house, in the kitchen with her tea, overlooking her extensive gardens. She loved to grow things.

"Yea, I found him and we're enjoying the nice weather while it lasts. I didn't know there were storms coming." He glanced at Ephyra, wondering if this was significant. She looked worried at the mention of the change in weather. How powerful was this merman sea monster?

"I didn't want to bother you two, but can I speak to Marcus? I want to see if he's coming home for Thanksgiving this year, you know how much advance notice he needs," she asked with a grim chuckle. Marcus hardly ever made it to any holiday but Christmas. Since it was nearly September, Gabriel couldn't fault her for asking now.

"He's actually out running some errands but I'll have him call you when he gets back."

Gabriel motioned for Ephyra to stay put while he left his ear to the cell phone. He climbed out on to the deck of the boat where Jake stood, alert and ready, holding his weapons. He motioned leaving and Jake nodded.

"Mom, I have to go, now," he interrupted her happy chatter. "Thanks for calling and I'll give you a heads up when I'm coming back. Maybe I can talk him into Thanksgiving, all right?" He smiled, knowing she'd hear it in his voice.

"Oh, that would be wonderful. Have fun, dear." Gabriel put the phone in his pocket and wondered what she'd say if he brought home a mermaid. He grinned—she'd probably be delighted. Their father had imparted his love of the sea to the entire family.

Gabriel headed toward the nearest hot dog stand.

# Chapter Twenty-Seven

Scyllane slipped the chains off her wrists and around her tail. She wiggled experimentally and her tail had enough strength to move her. She held out the mirror, now turned into a weapon. It seemed to weep over her tail, over her now empty egg pouch. Soft beads of pale light dripped from its surface and she felt the puffiness recede, the pain subside. The mirror didn't cure it but the wound didn't throb anymore.

"Perhaps you know what it's like to be barren," she whispered conspiratorially. It wasn't unusual for enchanted objects to harbor old souls. But the mirror just shined back her. She gripped it for courage and swam a short distance to one of the holes in the wall of the cavern. She slipped through the hole and couldn't decide which she wanted more: her freedom or revenge.

She spied Sevag and hate rose in her to smolder just beneath the surface. Scyllane felt the mirror begin to vibrate in her hand, its surface shining and the point sharp. She swam out of the cavern and toward the surface where Sevag was playing with weapons. The water became lighter and she felt currents swirling around ferociously. Scyllane imagined what the tides were like up above, imagined the clouds twisting into funnels of fury. She called to its power and the water responded.

Like a shadowy bolt of lightning she launched herself at Sevag from the side, the mirror spear drawing blood from his shoulder. He shouted in pain and whirled to see his attacker. Scyllane had the satisfaction of seeing his eyes widen in surprise as she let out a shriek and plunged the spear again toward his heart.

He swerved to the side and drew out his knife. Sevag grinned nastily as they danced in a tight circle, their tails flickering like lightning as they parried. Scyllane felt her strength waning against his brute force.

Sevag came down hard on her arm and she felt it break.

"A nice attempt," Sevag taunted and swept around her.

Scyllane switched the mirror spear to her other hand and held her injured one to her side. She blocked out the pain as she focused on Sevag's scarred face.

"Why did you tell Erebos I was unfaithful to him?" she shouted and dodged his knife.

His tail whipped at her, the spines on it coming dangerously close to her face. She flared her own layered fins and blocked them.

"I had good information, bitch," Sevag spat and dodged her as she flew at his left side. The mirror spear drew a small cut in his side. Sevag narrowed his eyes.

Scyllane panted. Good information? "From who?"

She saw they were heading into a strong current. It swept them up and her head momentarily broke the surface. Scyllane glimpsed clouds dark with storm. She dove back down under the water but felt the current sweeping her up again. Sevag was struggling as well, his long thick tail thrashing like a shark's. Scyllane whipped around with her spear glinting in the dim light.

"Who was it?" she screamed and lunged at him, her face contorted in rage.

Sevag ducked just in time to feel her flying over his head, leaping out of the water and then crashing back in. He pivoted to try to stab her but she was too quick. He charged her and swiped at her broken arm, making contact as she screamed and darted away.

Scyllane suddenly felt the currents surging. She let it propel her up and leaped with it out of the water and high into the tempestuous air where she could look down like a hawk to spot her prey. He was a small shadow under the waves, fighting to stay down. Scyllane let out a piercing cry and folded her body to plunge faster and faster back beneath the churning waves.

Her spear catapulted down true and she felt it slice into Sevag's shoulder. Her force drove it down through his chest and he let out a gurgle of rage. Scyllane let the current drag her down and with it she maintained a death grip on the spear. It tore down through his chest and into his abdomen. Sevag writhed in pain and his blood formed a purple cloud around him.

Scyllane lifted the spear from his torso and came to float next to his face. She put hers close to his, her eyes boring into his clear blue ones.

"Don't worry, I'll let your brother know of your death," she hissed and swam away as he sank to the dark blue abyss.

## Chapter Twenty-Eight

"So, this weather is Erebos' doing?" Gabriel asked skeptically. He finished his first hot dog and reached for another. Jake and Ephyra munched on theirs pensively for a few minutes as all three watched the waves rolling bigger and bigger. Storm clouds were scattered in the distance.

"Probably," Jake finally answered. "He's most likely pissed off because he can't find Ephyra. He might already know she's on land."

"Maybe," Ephyra sighed.

Gabriel saw her face and wanted nothing more than to take her away.

"Tortola is an island, we can't take you there. I think we should avoid the water," he said quickly forming a plan. "We still have over three days. I'm taking you home."

There was stunned silence.

"Home?" Jake demanded.

"Yes, to my apartment in Chicago. Jake, you're invited, too," Gabriel said but the merman shook his head.

"I'll stay. I don't think running away will help. He'll find her."

"I want to go, Jake. He's right, Scyllane gave me this time on land to find a champion and I shouldn't be near water where Erebos' spies can find me," Ephyra said seriously.

Gabriel was on his phone changing his flight and adding a seat. Marcus would have to fend for himself and Gabriel wasn't too concerned. His brother could come track him down if he wanted. Maybe Marcus could even go to their original plan on Tortola and keep an eye out there.

# Chapter Twenty-Nine

Gabriel inhaled the familiar scent of home, relieved they'd make it from Miami to Chicago without incident. Ephyra had been terrified for most of the flight and then exhausted. He settled her on his couch but her eyes were alert now, taking in his simple set up of the townhouse. Marcus had left a voice message, saying cryptically that he was making Jane was safe. He sounded frazzled. Gabriel called him as soon as they'd gotten in his apartment door, but got his voicemail. He relayed the change of plan.

Gabriel grabbed her bag of clothes from the living room floor and moved it to his spare bedroom. It wasn't big but it contained a queen-sized bed and a nightstand. Ephyra followed him in, flicking the lights on and off at the switch. He thought it was cute that she was still amazed at electricity.

"I can smell something different in here," she said curiously.

"You have a good nose. I try to keep it clean, but you probably smell Dag. He's my dog, the one thing missing here," Gabriel chuckled. "He likes to sleep on this bed but don't worry, I'll shut the door."

"Oh, a dog!" Ephyra said with a nod. "I have smelled them on shore many times. Is yours very large?"

"Dag's a Labrador retriever, so if your definition of large is about ninety-pounds, then yes," he said with a smile. He'd have to make arrangements yet to pick Dag up from the kennel.

"Unless you don't want a dog here," he added to her. Ephyra shrugged with a smile.

"I've never met one."

"You'll like him and even if you don't, he'll love you." Dag was pretty friendly to anyone, true to his Lab nature.

"Are you hungry?" he asked but she had moved on, exploring the other rooms.

"Where do you sleep?"

Ephyra was in his bedroom and Gabriel liked the way she fit there.

"Here." He smiled at the large bed covered in black sheets and bedspread, a sparse nightstand, stereo and adjoining bathroom. How good it would be, sleeping in his own bed tonight, he thought.

"Where did you get this?"

Ephyra went to the dresser where a conch shell sat glimmering, rimmed with silver.

"My dad found it and gave it to me, along with a whopping tale that I now think is true."

"I put the silver on this," she said in a hushed voice. Gabriel came to stand behind her.

"I'm sure he didn't know it belonged to anyone. You can have it back," he said gently.

Ephyra turned to him and smiled.

"No, it's yours. It's just odd that you ended up with it."

"My dad told me he'd seen a mermaid that day and this was his souvenir from the other world," Gabriel said nostalgically.

"He was right," she laughed.

Gabriel heard the doorbell ring and left Ephyra to answer it. His neighbor, a petite brunette was on his step. What was her name? He couldn't remember.

"I thought you'd been back a while," the woman was apologizing. "I didn't realize it was just this afternoon!"

"Yep, just got back." Gabriel felt Ephyra around the corner, listening. He didn't want her to get the wrong impression.

"Well, I have some dinner in the oven if you want to eat in, say, an hour?" She smiled and wiggled her body closer.

"That's great, but I'm sorry, I have some unpacking to do," Gabriel said politely.

Kim, that was her name. Gabriel said goodbye and closed the

door. He turned to Ephyra who was trying unsuccessfully to look neither jealous nor anxious.

"Sorry, that was my neighbor, Kim," he explained.

"She seemed to like you. Will you take her for a mate?" Ephyra asked boldly.

Gabriel stood shocked for a moment and then he understood. Women, even half-human women, had the same tendencies.

"No. I don't want her as my 'mate,'" he said and tried not to smirk.

"Oh," she said and turned away.

Gabriel milked the moment for a few seconds. Hadn't she been the one to say they couldn't be together?

"Well, maybe I can show you how humans pick a mate," Gabriel said teasingly. "Would you like to go on a date tomorrow night?"

Ephyra swung around and her eyes sparkled.

"I've read about dates," she said breathlessly. "They sound complicated. I don't know if you'd like to go on a date with me."

Gabriel laughed.

"There's no one I'd rather go on one with. It's kind of a human ritual to date first and usually sleep together later, I guess I rushed this."

"I didn't know there was a sequence, so it's like a spell?" she asked.

"Kind of. I just meant that some human women prefer to know the guy they would sleep with beforehand."

"This sleeping, this is what we did on the boat?"

"Um, yes," Gabriel said and was very aware of the fact they were alone in his house. He turned and opened the fridge for something to do.

"Sour milk, some eggs, and gross looking salad. I think I should grocery shop," he said with a sigh. He'd never been much of a cook himself and usually subsisted on spaghetti and frozen dinners.

"What is that?" Ephyra asked and peered into the fridge. She equated the refrigerator to the same kind of cold stones they had back home. It kept some of their food cool as well if they needed but most merfolk lived on live food.

"Big store filled with food. How about I leave you here for a couple hours and I'll be back with the dog too."

"Okay," Ephyra agreed.

Gabriel showed her how to lock and unlock the door and turned on the TV. He smiled as he saw her dozing in front of it. She was already the picture of an American human. Too bad she couldn't stay that way.

## Chapter Thirty

Marcus stared pensively out the third floor window of a random hotel he'd booked under a different name. Rain splattered against the thick glass and he could feel the humidity even inside.

He turned back to Jane and saw her sleeping, her face at peace. Jake entered the room eerily quiet. The merman had been sullen but helpful in staying. Jake had kept an ear out for news of the drug dealers and took shifts guarding Jane. Marcus didn't fool himself thinking Jake did it as a friend. He was probably just groping for an excuse to keep busy since Gabriel had whisked Ephyra away. It was clear his feelings for Ephyra went deeper than that of an old chum protecting a mermaid.

"He knows," Jake said simply and went to the large picture window, raising the blinds.

"Who? Who knows what?" Marcus returned irritably.

"Erebos knows the princess is not in the ocean anymore."

"Wait, princess?" Marcus stopped his pacing. "Ephyra is a princess?"

Jake turned to him slightly.

"She did not inform you." It was a quizzical statement. "Yes, she is the daughter of two realms, her purpose to unite them. Erebos seeks to destroy this unity. He may be on land as we speak. How far is this place Gabriel has taken her?"

"Chicago is thousands of miles from here, nowhere near the ocean. That was the plan wasn't it?" Marcus answered, his head spinning even more if that were possible.

Ephyra was a princess, a mermaid princess. He shook his head; he'd betrayed her friend, too. He was surprised she hadn't struck him down yet.

"The water is rising. It will overtake the land," Jake said matter of factly.

Marcus started with a jolt and ran to the window. He couldn't see the ocean very well but the weather outside was normal thunderstorm commotion.

"Do you mind not panicking me like that?" he said darkly and checked Jane.

Her eyes were open and he came to her side.

"Hey, babe, how do you feel?" He tenderly touched her cheek. He felt wet moisture on his hand and saw she was tearing up.

"I shouldn't have let you do that to her. I feel terrible," Jane said miserably.

"Shhh, I know," he soothed. Jake wondered if Muriel could ever forgive him.

"We need to get out of this place, because Jake says it will fall into the waves," he said and held out a hand to help her up.

Jake gave them a hard look with his golden eyes.

"I don't know how long Erebos can travel on land. He'll take the ocean with him," Jake said cryptically.

"Whatever. I don't need to understand. What I need is a way to destroy this Egregious," Marcus raked his hands through his hair in frustration.

"Erebos." Jake smiled acerbically.

They looked out the window just as sirens started sounding. Jake covered his ears and grimaced. Marcus flipped the remote and aimed it at the TV. The weather station statically came to life and he saw harried reporters babbling about the storm.

"A hurricane warning has been issued for the following counties . . . "

"Oh my God." Marcus sighed. He heard the rain against the glass, only now it sounded like bullets trying to shatter it.

"Let's get out of here. I'll call Gabe and let him know that nowhere's safe."

## Chapter Thirty-One

Dag bounded through the door and instantly circled his home, sniffing and wagging his tail like a humming bird's wings. The yellow Lab found Ephyra instantly and she nearly jumped off the couch at his exuberant greeting.

"Dag, down!" Gabriel shoved the dog off. "Sorry, he's harmless but a little excitable."

Ephyra laughed at the dog's curiosity, not unlike her own. He was just the thing to take her mind temporarily off the ticking time bomb that was her situation.

"Dag," she said and the ears pricked up. His blocky face was riveted on hers and Gabriel smiled.

"What does he do?" she asked and Gabriel laughed. He unwrapped the raw steak from the package and opened a bag of frozen vegetables.

"Well, mostly he sleeps and plays with his ball," Gabriel said fondly.

"So he doesn't hunt for you or protect you?" Dag thrust his muzzle under her arm.

"Not really. He'll bark at strangers but I think he'd just show a burglar the way in rather than attack him," Gabriel joked. "Some people have dogs that do jobs like guarding and search and rescue but I just like Dag for company."

"Oh, there are different races then," she said with a nod.

"Sure, dogs come in all sizes and shapes like people or mermaids, I suppose." He smiled at her and stirred the rice dish he was attempting to make. Gabriel had his cuts of steak ready to grill on his small patio that included a tie out for Dag.

Gabriel watched Ephyra, who watched the dog. He smiled as the Lab made a circle and flopped down on his bed by the TV.

Ephyra was enthralled.

"Do you have pets back home?" Gabriel asked from the kitchen.

"Pets?"

"Like Dag. An animal that you just have with you."

"Not exactly. Most of the sea life I know would follow me if I wanted but then they wouldn't be living like they're supposed to."

"Well, tell me about the kinds of animals you get to talk to," he suggested.

"I mostly enjoy speaking with whales, except orcas—they're rather moody. I love the angelfish, butterfly fish, rock beauties . . . I don't know what else you call some of them," she said apologetically. "We try to study human terms and language but it's difficult with limited resources."

"I only know some names because of my father."

"Does your mother also like the sea?"

"She does but I think it scares her, too," he said ruefully.

"She sounds wise then," Ephyra said. "Mermaids die all the time from natural causes in the water."

"So, about land monsters," Gabriel asked and put the lid on the pot. "I'm really not much help there."

"I can't figure it out either. Maybe Scyllane just wanted me to hide from Erebos." Ephyra sighed.

Gabriel didn't pry since she seemed apprehensive again. She was probably thinking about how to circumvent Erebos. He wished he were more help.

"We don't have much time but we have some. We'll find a way," he said firmly.

He heard something about Miami on the TV, and Gabriel stepped out of the kitchen to turn up the volume.

" . . . have declared a state of emergency. Citizens are advised to evacuate their homes . . . " the reporter was saying, a frown on her pretty face.

"What happened? We were just there," he said aghast. The

damage showed trees knocked over, houses decimated and, worst of all, walls of water crashing over the shore.

Ephyra put her hands to her mouth, in shock.

"This is my fault! I have to go back, right now!" she cried and stood. Dag began barking at her and Gabriel shushed him.

"I thought we agreed it wasn't safe."

"It isn't, but the only way to stop him is to surrender," she told him, fear clouding her eyes. "Maybe I can offer him a bargain. He'll drown the entire state, Gabriel."

Gabriel looked at her skeptically.

"Let's think about this," he said, trying to calm her. "This is routine for them—residents in Florida are always prepared for hurricanes." He sat her down and put her hand in his.

"You think is just a regular storm?"

They were interrupted by Gabriel's phone. He flipped it open and heard Marcus's voice covered with static.

" . . . it's getting bad here, I think you should bring her back. Jake says Erebos . . . do you believe . . . shit . . . "

The line went dead. Gabriel sighed. It looked like his happy future wasn't mean to be.

"That was Marcus. I think you're right," he told Ephyra and she looked up at him with soft eyes.

"Dammit, I was stupid to promise I could help you!" Gabriel looked around at his inadequate apartment and stupid meal. How was this helping solve the problem of a warlord hell bent on finding Ephyra?

"Gabriel, please stop," Ephyra pleaded as she followed him into the kitchen.

He turned to her with bright eyes.

"You've helped more than you know. I just have to return to the sea and hope Erebos will accept a bargain." She touched her lips softly to his.

Gabriel felt the familiar heat and it comforted him. She was all he wanted, royalty, mermaid or whatever. She was more than

Ephyra snuggled closer to him and Gabriel inhaled her scent.

"I'll take you back." Gabriel held her for as long as he could. His mind wandered through several scenarios where he either shot Erebos or ripped his head off.

# Chapter Thirty-Two

*Ephyra pushed seaweed out of her way and glimpsed her friend just beyond. She smiled and waved. Muriel just stood silent and sullen. Ephyra felt a shadow pass over her and suddenly tentacles shot out to grab Muriel. They dragged her down into a crevice, her screams bubbling. Ephyra swam hard and dove into the dark hole.*

*She didn't see anything but felt the thickness of blood around her, coating her hair and then washing out. There was a shrieking like souls being dragged into the underworld. Ephyra felt a tentacle starting to wrap itself around her waist and screamed before she catapulted out of the crevice.*

Ephyra jolted awake and looked wildly around her. The room spun and she felt sheets twisted around her. She breathed out in relief and untangled herself. She wasn't under the water, but it had been good to feel her form again. Ephyra missed her tail, and the ease of moving around.

She laid back and closed her eyes. Gabriel had taken Dag out for a walk and to drop him off at the sitter's house again so the house was quiet. They were leaving in a few hours. Ephyra was glad he'd taken her request seriously and even though his ideas were far-fetched, she loved him for trying to find a warrior that could fight Erebos.

Ephyra lost herself in thinking of Gabriel—what it would be like to live with him, to love him. Her body ached almost as much her heart at the thought of loving him. He was different from anything she'd expected. He was warm, kind and unafraid of her. Ephyra grinned as she thought of how she'd first treated him, and how he just waited for her to calm down.

She felt a warm hand on her thigh and a soft voice.

"Here you are."

Ephyra smiled, eyes still closed, wishing he'd slide that hand higher up her thigh. He'd been slowly showing her the pleasure of her human form. The hand gently stroked her leg and she felt the press of lips against her calf. She wiggled in delight and reached to take his hand.

The hands steadily caressed her legs, exploring every inch of them and kissing them. She groaned as she felt his head hover her stomach. Suddenly, Ephyra felt something wrong. Her eyes darted open to see an unfamiliar face with shaggy black hair and beady black eyes shining down at her. She opened her mouth to scream but a hand clamped over it.

Ephyra tossed and thrashed, trying to throw this man off, but his weight pinned her down. She angrily fought his embrace but he steadily held her until she was still. He took the hand off her mouth carefully and then shifted so that he straddled her.

"Who are you?" she shouted. She desperately hoped Gabriel was close to returning. She scanned the room for a weapon but saw nothing except a book on her stand.

"I recognize you in this form—you don't know me?" His voice taunted.

Ephyra felt a foreboding that shook her to the core.

"Erebos," she whispered, ashamed her voice quivered.

His dark eyes lit with a ghostly delight and he smiled to reveal sharp teeth. It was as if the transformation hadn't quite been completed. Some of the teeth were flat but most of them were pointed. Stringy hair was pulled back into a pony tail but strands escaped around his gaunt face.

"In the flesh," he said and sat back slightly. She shivered to feel him on her skin, wishing she'd kept the sheet on.

"How did . . . " she stopped asking a stupid question. It didn't matter how he'd found her but what happened now.

"I have spies with both fins and wings, darling. I knew Scyllane was hiding something from me but even she now understands that nothing can be hidden from me."

"Is she alive?" Ephyra attempted to slide out from under him but he pushed her back.

"She's as well as can be, once sterilized," he responded casually.

"Bastard!" Ephyra cried and thrust fists at him. Erebos caught them and laughed.

Ephyra angrily stopped struggling.

"In case you hadn't noticed, I can't go back," she said icily.

"Then you will either drown or be changed by Scyllane's good grace." He gazed down at her and saw her resolve instantly.

"Then I'll drown," Ephyra spat.

"Or I have a proposal of sorts, pet," he crooned. "I will spare your life in exchange for your bond to me."

Ephyra did a double take and her eyes widened.

"You would choose me for a mate?" she asked, bewildered. "I'm not full blood."

"I know, but it'd be such a shame to waste this," he motioned to her. "And my laws will allow several mates at once so if your sons are weak, then I will have others to choose from. Besides, the Coral people will be so heartened to hear you endorse my campaigns that perhaps they will finally stop fighting."

"They will never stop fighting you," she said. "I would never give them false hope."

Erebos looked at her with an amused expression.

"You're just like your father but with your mother's beautiful face, you know," he said and reached out to caress her face.

"Don't speak of them!" she shouted and tried to sit up again.

Erebos grabbed both her arms and pinned them above her head. His face was inches from hers as he inhaled her scent.

"You have a chance to come home, princess, I suggest you take it," he said smoothly. Ephyra could tell he was savoring the moment, taking his time like only a confident captor could.

"I have nothing there if you're the king." She turned her head away.

Erebos jerked her head to meet his eyes. She tried to disguise her emotions but he was reading them as if they were written on her face.

"You have found someone on land?" he whispered disgustedly. "You think you could be happier here . . . in love?"

Ephyra tried to keep tears from welling in her eyes. To hear it out loud made it more real than she ever admitted. Her thoughts went to Gabriel and she desperately wanted to protect him from this nightmare.

"Who is this creature you've decided is better than your own kind? A human."

"I haven't found anyone," Ephyra shot back at him.

"You are a disgrace to the two lines whose blood you carry!" he hissed and rage filled his body.

He slapped her hard across the face and Ephyra cried out at the pain. She tasted blood and then screamed as he bit her neck.

"You admit the Corals are a line then," she panted, hoping if she angered him enough he'd give her a swift death. She offered a silent apology to all her friends and to Gabriel, she had failed them all.

"You may have inferior blood in one half but it's merblood nonetheless. It's unthinkable for you to take a human mate," Erebos roared. He looked at her smoldering eyes. "Let's see how much you enjoy it."

He tore the sheet in strips and bound her wrists to the bedposts. Ephyra freed her legs and kicked out. Erebos grunted as he caught one in his gut. He shoved them aside and covered her body with his, thrusting himself between her legs.

Ephyra cried out as he tore her shirt to bare her breasts to him. He nipped them hard. She tried to block out the pain and he smothered her under his weight. He used his sharp teeth to draw blood; she felt the stickiness tricking down her breasts and her stomach.

She tried to feel for any give in the twisted sheets, but they cut into her wrists. Her legs were heavy and useless, pinned beneath him. His teeth gashed her stomach and she writhed in pain.

A warm hand groped her breasts, tasting the blood and suckling at their peaks. Then she felt a rough finger touch her between her legs. Ephyra bucked in terror as it shoved inside her and explored. She wondered if he intended to sterilize her like Scyllane. Ephyra realized she would die because human female eggs were not in the same place as a mermaid's.

"I'm quite familiar with human torture, my dear," he panted.

Ephyra's scream stuck in her throat, her humiliation complete as she lay helplessly. Tears cascaded down her cheeks and she desperately tried to think of Gabriel. This was nothing like it had been with him as Erebos pushed her legs apart like sea kelp.

"What the hell!" Gabriel's shout made her eyes pop open and she tried to warn him.

Gabriel had already launched himself at Erebos and grabbed his shoulder, throwing him off the bed and slamming him into her nightstand. Erebos quickly leaped up and squared with his opponent. The man's eyes blazed in fury and more than that, fear for her. Erebos nearly laughed out loud.

"This is your human?" he sneered toward Ephyra.

Ephyra began to shake uncontrollably, afraid for Gabriel. He was staring coldly at Erebos and then moved forward, punching the other in the face. Erebos moved aside, his nose bleeding.

Gabriel hastily unbound her. He made a quick check and saw blood on her torso. His eyes turned a dark shade of menace.

Ephyra saw him grab the nearest post of the bed and snap it off. Whirling, he swung it as hard as he could. Erebos dodged the first but was surprised when the second hit him across the jaw and he fell.

Uncontrolled anger filled the room and Erebos got up to swing a fist at Gabriel in return. He ducked. Erebos swung again, using his legs to lash out as well. Gabriel grunted at the impact in his abdomen and fell to his knees. He took a hardcover book and thrust it up, corner first, into Erebos as he leaned over to punch again.

The corner jabbed into Erebos' stomach and he grimaced. He

grabbed Gabriel's hair. Gabriel panted as he was pulled to his feet, then lashed out with a left side kick and connected with Erebos' chest. The other had the wind knocked out of him and let go. Gabriel didn't stop but kept pummeling him with his fists until he couldn't tell if it was his blood or the intruder's.

Ephyra had swung from panic to awe at Gabriel's fighting skill. He should have been dead by now but Erebos was winded and looking frustrated. Over and over the warlord slammed the man into the wall and Gabriel kept getting up. He swung, kicked, and dodged.

"Stop, please!" Ephyra cried as Erebos once more knocked Gabriel into the wall with his power. "I have a champion to claim!"

Erebos stopped his fist, his other hand around Gabriel's throat and then threw him to the side. His hair had come loose and stuck to his face, his mouth open and panting. Ephyra realized Erebos had almost lost the fight as Gabriel got back up. It shook something in her and she realized she'd underestimated Gabriel.

Ephyra felt a jolt of power; the champion curse gave her a small bit back. She used it to try to summon a banishing spell against Erebos. She saw Gabriel's eyes flashing fire and his knee coming up to crash into the warlord. The impact threw them both against the wall. The Shoal leader cried out in fury. He summoned all the power he had, growled a spell and hurled it at Gabriel. The man crumpled at his feet, writhing in pain.

"Who would stand against me?" Erebos growled.

Ephyra put herself in front of him but saw Gabriel was getting up again, spitying blood from his mouth. He lunged like a torpedo, flying past her and tackling the man again, shoving him against the wall, his elbow in the hollow of his throat.

"Me," he gasped. "She chose me for her champion!" Gabriel stared with hard eyes into Erebos' murky black ones.

Erebos stilled.

"No human can undo a spell," he whispered with narrowed eyes.

"Just get the fuck away from her," Gabriel snarled.

Ephyra stood stunned, half the sheet draped around her body. She felt her heart tear in two at what Gabriel had done. She wasn't sure if she was elated or devastated. The champion had rules of its own—ones she hadn't known were pertinent to tell him. She felt tears slide down her face as she gazed at her champion, pinning her enemy like he was a crab against the wall.

"Then get ready to fight," Erebos snapped and shoved Gabriel off him.

Gabriel wiped the blood from his mouth. He glared at Erebos, and then went to stand next to Ephyra. She took his hand, palm up and held in one hand; with the other, she placed her fingernails into it. She removed them to leave a spiraling design with a sword in the middle.

"You are bound now. You are my champion," Ephyra said with agony in her voice.

"Now, go," Ephyra commanded Erebos and she shoved her spell toward him. Erebos lifted his lip at her before being vanishing, leaving only a small blood smear on the wall.

Gabriel paced furiously across the floor, his eyes glaring at the bloody bed. Ephyra remained standing.

"I'll kill him, why did you do that?" Gabriel exploded. "Where did he go?"

"We need time," Ephyra stuttered. Her mind was reeling with the consequences of what he'd done. She looked up at him with full eyes. "Why did you say you'll be my champion?"

Gabriel stopped pacing and tilted her face up, his hands gentler than she expected.

"Because I didn't know what else to do," he laughed harshly. "I know it's impossible, but I love you. I want to help and if this is the only way then I'll die before he touches you again."

"I'll recover, I'm not even human, remember?" she said with an attempt at bravery.

Gabriel narrowed his eyes as he gazed at her. She knew he felt her courage and that it nearly ripped his heart out.

"Tell me what to do," he said simply.

Ephyra nodded through her tears. She gripped his hands in hers and pulled him closer. He had no idea that what he'd done would keep them apart more than the ocean.

"We have to train you and we will have to return to the ocean."

"We?" Gabriel raised a brow. Then he grimaced at the pain it caused.

"Jake knows the ways of mermen. There's an arena far under water that all the ancient fights take place in."

"How am I supposed to fight under the water," Gabriel grunted.

"Let me clean you up first and we'll talk about it later."

He followed her to the bathroom where she soaked towels in warm water and gently wiped his cuts.

"I can do this," he said, but she sat him down on the toilet lid.

"Please, let me." Gabriel complied. He peeled off his shirt and she gasped at the bruising that already marred his skin.

"Are any of your bones broken?"

"Don't think so."

Ephyra was glad to feel her power returning slowly and summoned a healing spell. His eyes started to close and she hastily helped him to his bed. He would need to heal quickly. She closed her eyes against the pain that awaited them.

# Chapter Thirty-Three

Jake felt like a lightning bolt hit his head and he bent over, clutching his temples.

"What's wrong?" Marcus cried and stopped the car.

"Wait," he panted.

Jake saw the sea witch's face in his mind and realized she wanted to communicate. She was saying something, her words becoming clearer. She was telling him to stop resisting and the pain would subside. He did.

"Has she found a warrior?" Scyllane's voice came into his head like a fog horn.

"No," Jake said in his mind. Scyllane frowned.

"Erebos was on land but I can't feel him anymore."

"How?"

"I'm not the only one with access to the ancient runes, Jake. You need to come back, I can't hold two spells at once like this for much longer," she said, irritated with her own limited power.

"I need a few minutes. I'm guiding two humans."

"What are you doing wasting your time?" she demanded.

"Ephyra wanted her friends taken care of, no matter how stupid."

"I see you're as under her thumb as ever," Scyllane complained. "Very well, you have an hour and Ephyra has twenty-four hours. Make sure you get near water."

Suddenly she was gone from his mind. He straightened to face two sets of anxious eyes staring at him.

"The spell is dissolving, I have to return and Ephyra needs to be in the water in twenty-four hours."

"I called Gabe but the reception was spotty. I'll text him to make sure." Marcus paused, considering the merman. "I'm sorry for what I did to Muriel, and I know it probably doesn't mean anything to you but I had to say it."

"It doesn't, you're right. You should say it to her but you'll never see her again. I will relay your message though if it's important to you," Jake said mildly. He couldn't condone Marcus' behavior but he also knew he was just human and he couldn't possibly understand.

"Please," Marcus said and held out his hand. "You make a great human." Jane gave him a hug.

"Good luck," Jake told them as they got into their car.

He lifted his head to the wetness pouring from the sky. It felt good after being so dry and he turned his gaze toward the frothing ocean. He wanted to be back home. Jake closed his eyes and sat down on a rock that stood against the relentless slashing of waves. He prayed Ephyra would return soon—he was a fool to have let her out of his sight. He decided he'd offer himself to be champion and one way or another they'd put an end to this madness.

## Chapter Thirty-Four

The queen angelfish nibbled on Scyllane's fin and woke her from a garish dream. She sat up and the fish whispered in her ear. Scyllane frowned to hear Erebos had returned. She thanked the angel with some scraps of shrimp.

Scyllane could feel her mind sliding closer to insanity. She was out of hope now and the mirror was her only friend. She smiled at it, the glinting object silent but close.

She unwrapped her tail around herself and flexed her fins. They were still somewhat sore but still functioning. It was time. Scyllane gathered every bit of magic she had left to her, grabbed the mirror, and asked for Erebos.

Her estranged husband's furious face glared at her through the surface. She saw Sevag's mangled body in the background and a smile lit her face. Erebos was ready for her now but she couldn't swim quickly in her state. Scyllane gave a sharp call and a giant squid loomed up from the depths, its huge eye luminescent and roving.

"To the palace," she said to it and the beast floated to her.

Scyllane grabbed the notch of hard skin on its back and the squid shot in the direction of the palace. Within minutes, she saw tiers rising in the distance and something else that she hadn't seen in centuries. Spires of black rock twisted around a circular ring and guards were hard at work moving rock out of the middle. She reined in the squid and they hovered for a moment. Scyllane realized Erebos wasn't simply back, he was recreating the arena.

"She's found a warrior," she whispered and felt hope burst through her chest.

Scyllane felt like shouting in triumph but one of the guards lifted an alarm as he spotted her. She cursed her slowness as she urged the squid to run. Mermen surrounded her from every side and plunged their spears into the beast. He gave a cry and bucked Scyllane off. She flew to the side, into arms covered in hard armor.

Scyllane blasted the ring of mermen with her magic and it flung them back. She groaned at her bad luck—the magic's light was like a beacon and she saw a black Shoal coming toward her.

"No one harms her. You will answer for murder," Erebos' enraged shout came to her and Scyllane froze.

She turned, mirror spear at the ready and threw flashes of power into the black current. It scattered, but she saw Erebos' tall form glide out of it, his eyes red with grief. Scyllane felt him sliding invisible threads of a magic net around her and she instantly combated it. The net pulled tighter until she was forced to stop struggling and drop the mirror, where it floated away.

Scyllane jutted her chin defiantly and her eyes bore into his.

"You are the only thing keeping Ephyra in human form, aren't you?" Erebos said, answering his own question.

Scyllane growled at him. He knew if she died, her spell died with her and it would force Ephyra to come sooner.

"Keep her alive within two breathes," he said to the guards and floated away.

Scyllane felt the net dissolve but a dozen mermen closed in on her and she could feel her powers draining. The mirror couldn't help her anymore. She tried to call it, to see where it had gone but all she saw was a dull gold gleam far below.

## Chapter Thirty-Five

"Gabriel!"

Gabriel's head shot up and he sprinted to the bathroom where he saw her frozen in confusion.

Points of spines poked their heads out from her wrist to elbow and she pulled up her pant leg to show him shiny scales. They were beautiful, but Gabriel knew it wasn't a good sign.

"Something's happened," she whispered in anguish. "I thought we had more time."

Gabriel gave her hand a squeeze. He had his suitcase still packed, but knew he probably wouldn't need it where they were going.

"It's all right, our timetable will just move up. Flights into Florida are canceled, they're under a hurricane warning, so we're driving."

"I expect nothing less of a champion," Ephyra tried to joke.

They scrambled to get in the car. Gabriel had dropped Dag off at the sitter's with a quick apology. The car sped down I-90 and Gabriel pushed the speed limit.

"I may be in over my head, princess, so let's go over this plan to get me in the water."

Ephyra removed a blue moonstone from her pocket and held it out. It sparkled in the sunlight and changed colors from teal to cerulean to deep navy.

"What's that?" Gabriel vaguely remembered Muriel wearing something like that.

"It's how you will breathe under water," Ephyra said wryly. "The moonstone has the power to grant you another form. That's why Muriel was able to become human."

"So, I'm supposed to turn into a mer . . . person?" he asked and tried to maintain their straight path. Wearing a woman's piece of jewelry was one thing but that it would turn him into a merman was another.

"Yes, I think it has to touch your skin," Ephyra answered sensibly.

Gabriel's heart was racing. He tried to picture his legs disappearing and couldn't do it.

"Whatever it takes." He gave Ephyra a grim smile, the urge to kill Erebos still strong in his breast.

The car sped even faster as the shadows raced the sun.

*

Jake felt the tingling in his arms and legs. He watched as his legs began to fuse into one. He recognized the pattern of his scales merging the joints together, his knees disappearing. Jake quickly dove from the rock into the water; it closed over his head like a blanket. He hoped Ephyra had not changed yet. For some reason, he just knew Gabriel would get her to the water in time. It both hurt and reassured him.

He felt power rush to his lower half and looked down to see his tail flexing and muscular. The split fins propelled him with ease through the currents and away from the shore. Jake was so glad to be back home, he felt like spinning. But the feeling quickly subsided as he saw a perpetual gloom of fragments of houses and scattered merfolk.

Jake tore his shirt off and let it float away. He examined his body to make sure it was his. His broad shoulders and wide chest were the same, his torso muscled and supple. He swam cautiously through rubble and avoided dark holes. He spied a few of what appeared to be armed guards in the distance. The Coral realm was destroyed to a house and he wondered where they all had gone.

A cold hand reached up and he shied away in a flash only to recognize Muriel's drawn face coming up from a hole in the rocks. He swam back and grabbed her shoulders to pull her close.

"Are you hurt?" he asked worriedly.

Muriel was thin and her usual vibrant color was gone. She was a shadow of what she should have been.

"I'm sorry, Muriel," he murmured. She clung to him for a moment with bony hands and then drew back. He couldn't imagine what she went through.

"You shouldn't be seen with me," she whispered and they sank a bit lower into the shadows.

"I don't care. What you did was not a sin as they would have you think, Muriel," Jake told her firmly.

"I wanted to love him," she sobbed, her hair sweeping across her face. "I was a fool."

Jake rubbed her hand softly.

"It was your decision." He relayed Marcus' apology and saw Muriel smile sadly. She looked at him with wounded but clear eyes.

"What are you doing back?" Muriel said and averted her gaze. Jake could tell she was embarrassed.

"Scyllane's spell is broken. She warned me it would happen but not this quickly. I fear something's happened to her. Ephyra should be coming back."

"I haven't heard from Scyllane. All I know is that the arena is being built again," Muriel said hollowly.

Jake swung around to her.

"The arena? Has a champion been declared?"

"Must have." Muriel shrugged. "I've seen the arena being constructed, big black spires and shaped like a pearl."

"Scyllane better be alive to keep Ephyra safe." Jake started to swim off. Muriel put a hesitant hand on his shoulder.

"Will you come back?" she asked, not daring to go further toward the realm borders.

Jake gave her a soft smile.

"Promise. If you see anything on the outskirts, don't challenge it," he said and with a flash of his tail he moved toward his future.

## Chapter Thirty-Six

"Can we go any faster?" Ephyra panted as more scales appeared on her legs.

Gabriel had a sudden vision of her as a lizard. He pushed it away with a dry grin—the exhaustion was getting to him.

"Yea, we just have to get gas first," Gabriel said as he pulled off on I-65. He'd been driving for more than nineteen hours and his eyes felt like sandpaper. Florida had never seemed so far away.

As the pump clicked off the fuel pouring into their tank, Gabriel stuck his head in the window and glanced down at her stretched out in the back seat. He visibly controlled his reaction. It was more the shock of seeing her half fused together and scales covering her legs. She grimaced in understanding.

"I've never been repulsed by my own figure."

"Don't be, you're beautiful. Do you need anything?"

Gabriel grabbed a soft blanket from the trunk and flung it across her legs. Ephyra thanked him gratefully.

"I'll be okay but I know you need sleep."

"I need to get you back," Gabriel answered and went into the store.

When he came back he saw how red his eyes were in the rear view mirror but determinedly he started the car again and jammed his foot on the accelerator.

"I'm sorry, Gabriel."

He glanced at and wanted to put his arms around her. Her face was pale and her luminous eyes were filled with unshed tears. Gabriel could tell she was in pain but she didn't complain. His heart swelled with pride at her resilience.

"There is nothing to be sorry about," he told her firmly.

Gabriel smiled and took a huge gulp of coffee. The hot liquid stung his throat but it kept him awake. The highway turned into a blur of lights as they sped through the night. The pavement was like a black serpent tongue and headlights started to look like fairies as Gabriel downed more and more caffeine. He checked on Ephyra often but she finally slept in the back seat.

He lovingly traced the curve of her jaw with his eyes, the flow of glorious ebony hair that cascaded past her breasts. Gabriel's mind was filled with thoughts that made his blood heat. There was so much he wanted to show her, teach her, make love to her. Gabriel sighed. He wasn't sure if he'd survive this champion fight. If she was safe at the end of it, it was enough for him. He understood more of himself through her than he'd ever known. That was a gift not everyone could say they had been given.

Gabriel set the cruise control at ninety-five, hoping any police were asleep in their cars. He checked the weather on his phone and saw the mass of red and yellow radar blotches were growing over Florida. They were closer by the hour despite gas and bathroom breaks.

"Gabriel?" Ephyra's voice broke through his reverie.

"Hey, hun, you okay?" He saw sweat beading on her forehead.

Ephyra smiled weakly.

"I think it's getting worse," she said and tossed the blanket off. She frowned at her bottom half. Her legs were now indistinguishable from each other and fins were splitting at what were her feet.

Gabriel slowed the car to pull over on the side of the road. He raced around and opened the door to lean in over her.

"What can I do?" he asked worriedly. For a moment, he was awed by her tail's color and silkiness. The transition was complete and it was no longer a shock—it was amazing. Gabriel didn't touch it but found he wanted to.

"I have a case of water, would that help?" he offered, motioning to a patch of flaking scale.

Ephyra smiled weakly.

"You always think of everything," she responded.

Gabriel gave her a small smile and opened the trunk to get the case of water. He opened a few bottles and poured them over the spot. Ephyra sighed at the wetness. It wasn't salty like the sea but it was cool and wet.

"Maybe I could soak the blanket," he suggested, not caring that his upholstery was getting wet.

He poured water all over the blanket and gently laid it over her tail. Gabriel felt his hand accidently brush her fins and drew his hand back as if it were hot.

"I don't want you to think I'm repulsive. You can touch me if you want," Ephyra said quickly and reached out for his hand.

Gabriel let her take it and guide back to her tail. He gulped when he felt its smoothness, the muscle beneath the intricately patterned scales. The color was radiantly green with swirls of red and gold, ending in almost translucent fins that felt harder than they looked.

"I'm not repulsed. I didn't want to hurt you," he said softly in wonder.

Ephyra sighed and laid back.

"You aren't, you couldn't ever do that," she said and closed her eyes. Gabriel wrapped her fins, shut the door, and slid into the driver's seat. The car rolled forward and they were again speeding south. Gabriel decided to head for Pensacola instead of driving all the way through the state. They needed to get to the ocean. He knew bottled water was not the same as the salt of the sea.

## Chapter Thirty-Seven

"Just a few more hours," Gabriel said and drained his cup. Oddly, he wasn't feeling tired anymore, just worried. Ephyra had been asleep for most of the ride so far, not even waking now when he stopped for gas.

It had seemed like years since they'd started the trip and Gabriel didn't know how he was functioning on no sleep. Instead, it was like his senses were heightened and his mind wouldn't stop buzzing. The rune on his hand may have contributed because he felt it warm and pulsing in his palm.

Ephyra's face popped up in the rear view mirror an hour later, her eyes bright and almost feverish.

"Hey, do you need me to soak the blanket again?" Gabriel asked but she shook her head.

"I can feel we're close." She leaned back.

They crossed the state line without incident and Gabriel sped up as if Erebos himself were behind them.

"Beach should be coming up soon. I hope no one's on it," Gabriel muttered.

Within the hour, the stretch of white sand appeared and they passed hundreds of cars in outbound traffic trying to get out of the state. Police were lined up, cars flashing red and blue on the hot pavement. Gabriel tuned in the radio and heard that south Florida including the Keys was in evacuation, due to hurricane conditions. He sighed. The storm was swirling in the distance but at the moment the sun was out and the heat radiated through the windows.

"Hang on, Ephyra," he said and turned the wheel.

He drove as far as he could to a small crescent beach in the city's outskirts and pulled into the parking lot. It would have to do even though there were a few people dotting the shoreline.

Gabriel shoved the keys in his pocket and raced to the side door.

"We're almost there. I'm going to carry you." He gently gathered Ephyra into his arms.

She nodded and clung to him with shaky arms. They both smelled the briny air and the roar of the waves assaulted their ears.

Gabriel felt the mark on his hand start to burn hotter the closer they got to the water's edge. It seemed to be pumping adrenalin into him and he found he was running effortlessly. Plunging into the cool of the ocean, he softly laid Ephyra in the waves, the blanket left behind on the sand.

Gabriel couldn't help but smile at her exuberance as the water refreshed her. Ephyra flipped her tail and the water splashed his face. She turned to him, holding herself on the bottom with her arms.

"Thank you." She smiled and he knelt in the waves in front of her.

"I wish you didn't have to come," she said sadly and handed him the necklace. The blue stone shone in the sunlight like a beacon. Gabriel felt compelled to take it.

"Why?" he asked and slipped the necklace on.

"Because as my champion . . . " Ephyra stopped, tears gathering in her eyes. Gabriel reached out to touched her face, the spray plunging around them.

"I told you, whatever I have to do." Her eyes tracked his with an intensity that Gabriel felt he could lose himself in.

"And for that there will never be another for my heart," she told him. "I have much to tell you now."

Gabriel didn't have much time to think about her cryptic meaning because the change happened in minutes. He gasped in surprise and felt his legs turning to jelly; he flopped over into the water and tried not to look as his legs fused together. There wasn't any pain but a tingling that was like when his foot fell asleep.

Suddenly, he had no feet and he saw two split fins sparkling in the sun. A third caudal fin waved behind him. The water washed over them and he saw his tail was a deep jade with the mark of the champion woven into the scales in gold. Scarlet sigils wound around the scales as well, giving it the appearance of deliberate scarring. His arms were covered in retractable spines, dark green with red tips. Retract, Gabriel thought, and to his delight, they did. The spines seamlessly shot back into tiny holes in his arm.

He felt the back of his head, underneath his hair, to find two sets of gills just as Jake had told him. Gabriel felt their feather softness covered by a hard shell. It was like touching a scab on the back of his head and he grimaced.

"Whoa," he said through a mouthful of water. He spat it out but noticed the saltiness was no longer offensive.

Gabriel glanced around to make sure no one was watching them. He smiled and flopped his tail experimentally, his hands still digging into the sand for balance. The powerful muscle splashed Ephyra in the face as she giggled and moved closer.

"You have a special gift," she said in admiration of the spines on his forearms.

"These?" He grinned and flexed them. "Just something I found lying around."

She giggled.

"I wasn't sure if the stone would differentiate species. It has given you the best of all the merfolk." Gabriel saw her watching him closely with a happy expression. He tried to push himself further into deeper water. The waves kept propelling him back to shore but his tail was heavy enough to keep him from beaching.

"Just concentrate on where you want to go," she told him with a grin.

Gabriel laughed as he flipped his tail hard and shot out to sea. Water closed over his head and he opened his eyes to see sand stirred in tornadoes and the waves crashing overhead. Ephyra guided him through the water. He peered into the cerulean blue water and saw sand swept around in rivulets, sea shells tossed in the current and schools of fish scattering.

"Can I talk to you under the water?" he asked and when he opened his mouth, he was surprised that he could. He realized that humans, no matter what their technology provided, could never live under the water.

"You're doing well," Ephyra answered and laughed. She lashed her tail and sped off at top speed. Gabriel almost lost track of where she went before she catapulted back to him.

"I need to learn how to do that."

He didn't wait for instruction but instead gave his tail a powerful thrust to see what would happen. Gabriel felt his body slim down, his fins tucked in at his side and he rocketed forward. He stopped just short of slamming into a coral bank. He pushed his hands out but his tail stopped him on a dime. Gabriel laughed as three yellow-tailed fish scattered.

The sun still shone here and its rays slanted into the water to illuminate the reef as if he were on hallowed ground. Gabriel marveled at how much more vibrant the colors were without goggles, no matter how clear. The fish weren't scared of him but nibbled at his chest and ears. Eels peeked out of their shelters to stare at him and a few stingrays passed by with waves of their fins.

"You look very natural," Ephyra's voice came up next to him.

He turned to her with a wide smile and noticed how even more beautiful she was in her true form. Blue-black hair clouded around her face, scales half covered her breasts and her tail was a gorgeous mix of blue, gold, and green.

"This is amazing." He swished his tail again. Ephyra followed and trailed her hand over his abdomen. Gabriel felt a tightening in his chest and pulled her closer. Ephyra laughed and they floated in each other's arms. She showed him the way back to her realm.

"Can we speak to them?" Gabriel spotted a blue whale. The gigantic mammal was peacefully heading in their direction.

"Not in this language but they understand in here," Ephyra said and pointed to her head.

Gabriel pushed forward and slid up to the side of the whale, its tiny black eye staring at him. He tried to think hard thoughts at the whale and the whale let out a low whistle. Gabriel smiled.

"She said okay!" Gabriel called to Ephyra and motioned her over.

"What did you ask?" She gazed at him curiously.

"We're getting a ride," Gabriel laughed and lay back on the whale's back. Ephyra followed, unable to deny his enthusiasm.

"We don't usually ask them to do this."

"I know, she said as much but I asked nicely," he responded and wedged himself in a bump on the whale's back. The whale turned around and started heading south.

"You just like to flirt with females no matter the species."

He laughed. "Is it working?"

Ephyra gave him a sideways glance. "I have an idea. I'll be right back," she said and dove off the whale.

Gabriel watched her disappear but stayed where he was, enjoying the ride. He watched the coral fade into deep rock beds and those plunge into dark abysses that he would have loved to explore without scuba gear. All different species of fish large and small passed by, on their way to eat, mate or both. He smiled when he saw a sail fin fish. That had been his father's favorite. *I only go as far as the next reef,* the whale's thoughts came into Gabriel's head. He nearly jumped in surprise.

*Thank you,* he responded. The whale bobbed her head slowly.

*There is danger ahead. Be sure you have friends in that area,* she said fretfully.

*Well, that's what I'm looking for,* Gabriel answered ruefully. It wasn't far from the truth. He had not forgotten that at the end of this journey a dark warlord waited for him.

*You are different, merman.*

*I've never spoken to a whale,* Gabriel thought back. *Do you have a name before we part?*

*What is a name?*

*Oh, I see. Like clicks right?* Gabriel thought about the sounds he'd heard of whales under water.

*I do not know what a click is but if it is your name, it is a good one,* the whale responded.

*No, Click should be your name. Would you mind if I called you that?*

*I would not mind. Farewell, merman. Protect your companion, she is in danger, too.*

*To my last breath.* Gabriel floated off the whale's back. She waved a flipper at him and then with a whoosh of her tail she went to surface for air.

Gabriel liked watching her large form from below, how it blocked the light like an ascending Greek god. He glanced down to see if Ephyra was back and saw her coming up to him. She held a leathery band of some sort.

"I named the whale Click," he said teasingly.

Ephyra raised an eyebrow.

"You named a whale?" she asked incredulously. "They don't have names, she told you that right?"

"I know, but she made an exception for me." Gabriel gave her an impish grin.

Ephyra rolled her eyes good naturedly.

"I made this to protect your forearms and also hold the stone so it doesn't slip off around your neck," she said and held out the bracer.

Gabriel's eyes lit up and he watched her fasten it on. There were holes for the spines to shoot through, and it was hard on the outside but flexible. She lifted his arm to his neck and placed the stone in the inside of the bracer where it stuck securely. She snapped the chain and let it fall away.

"There. Better?"

"Much." He impulsively kissed her.

He'd kissed a few girls in pools but it wasn't the same in the open ocean with Ephyra. The heat between them dispelled any cold currents and he felt his heart beating faster. She pulled away quickly though.

"What's wrong?" he asked and cupped her face.

"I, um, it's hard . . . "

"Ephyra, what is it? You don't think I can do this?"

Ephyra gave him a sad smile but shook her head. She took his hand and they started swimming again.

"It's not that. As champion there are certain rules," she began with a quiver. "Gabriel, if you beat Erebos, we can't be together."

"If?" was Gabriel's first thought followed by, "I figured on that. I'm not a mermaid, er man." He gave her a lopsided grin.

"That's the other thing . . . " Ephyra groaned. "As the champion victor, you would be condemned to remain in this form. There's only been one other who's done this and he rebelled, killed half the royal family to earn his freedom."

Gabriel drifted for a moment.

"I see," was all he said for a few minutes.

"I have a plan," Ephyra said in a rush. "If we can find Scyllane we can reverse the champion mark and you can go back. I am sure I can find someone else . . . "

Gabriel's face turned dark. "I'm not sure if you're insulting me or protecting me."

Gabriel let go of her hand and saw the hurt on her face.

"The champion is a slave, Gabriel. The title is fancy but the victor is still in my command, in my military services. He or she cannot be anything more than a protector of the realm. We could not be together in the way we want."

Gabriel mulled this over, his frown increasing. No more family, no teaching, no cars. Was this worth his life? He wanted to say it was but his own well-being and pride wouldn't let him. He glanced at his tail and sighed. Suddenly a lifetime of living underwater didn't seem as appealing as before. His future now held no family of his own, no free choice.

"What do you want me to do?" he asked simply and stopped,

floating. Ephyra turned to face him, her eyes clouded with anxiety.

"I want you to *not* sacrifice yourself for me," she whispered. "I didn't think being on land in your world would change me so much. I should have told you sooner but I didn't . . . I mean you weren't supposed to . . ."

"And what would I have to do if I lived as your slave?" Gabriel asked with steel in his voice.

"I wouldn't command you to do anything, but you wouldn't be able to leave," she responded brokenly.

"Well, I volunteered didn't I? I'm going to do this, even if you think I won't succeed," he said and turned away.

"Gabriel, that's not what I think!" Ephyra cried desperately and reached out for his arm. He slid just out of reach.

"Please," she whispered but he was far ahead, swimming with purpose.

Gabriel flashed his tail hard, trying to exert as much of his anger out on the currents of the water and not Ephyra. It wasn't her fault he'd fallen in love with her. He sighed. He knew she felt worse about it than he did.

A life as a merman couldn't be all that bad, he tried to convince himself, but he knew he wouldn't make it that long. Perhaps she could grant him one day to say goodbye to Marcus and his mother. Gabriel wondered how he could explain that.

He glanced back at Ephyra who was trailing miserably behind him. For a moment it seemed as if his heart were hanging out on his sleeve. Promise or not there was no way he'd ever not protect her. The love between them was far beyond what any physical barrier could stop. She was what was missing in him and he'd never understood that until now. She complemented him. To live as her slave would be better than not living with her at all.

Gabriel slowed a bit and let her catch up, then caught her hand in his. He gave her a slow, sad look, but it told her he was hers until the end. Ephyra's tears floated away and she crushed him in a hug. He savored her touch as long as he could.

# Chapter Thirty-Eight

The currents were getting stronger and Jake could guess that above the water the weather wasn't much better. He could sometimes hear thunder since they weren't in deep waters. Seaweed swayed briskly and fish took to hiding places. He only imagined what devastation Erebos was wreaking on the shores of the human realm.

Jake led the company of guards in a large loop that bypassed the main guard at the front of the palace. He knew parading in with only forty mermen wouldn't exactly impress Erebos. He wanted to go in the side pass and surprise the Shoal leader, give him a reason to think he didn't know the palace as well as those who lived there before.

"Who's that?" asked the merman to his right as he pointed his spear at two figures swimming quickly by the coral banks.

Jake squinted and tried to make out if they were armed. Then he caught the dark bloom of ebony hair and the gold spirals in a tail.

"Ephyra?" he called, hardly daring to believe his eyes. A rush of heat soared through him as he hurried toward her.

The mermaid instantly perked her head and called back with a smile. She rushed into his open arms and gave him a fierce hug. Jake then noticed the merman behind her and with a start recognized the human man. They regarded each other for a tense moment.

"Gabriel."

"Jake." Gabriel extended his hand. The mermen behind Jake murmured amongst themselves. Jake took the offered hand in a firm grip.

"Thank you for returning the princess safely," he dismissed Gabriel.

Gabriel gave Ephyra a sharp look and she stepped between them.

"Jake, he's here on my behalf."

"We don't need someone who doesn't know our customs, Ephyra. Erebos is building the arena and the battle will take place soon," he said and shuttled her a few feet away for a private conversation.

"We only have a few days remaining and I need your help. Are you a General?" she asked in confusion at seeing the badges on his uniform.

Jake smiled at her proudly.

"They sought me, they need my knowledge of the ancient laws and legends. I would like to ask you something though," Jake said and his eyes implored hers.

Ephyra nodded.

"I would pledge myself your champion and will fight for your throne," he said solemnly and lowered his eyes.

"Jake, I . . ." Ephyra stammered and saw his face fall slightly.

"Am I unworthy?" he asked tightly.

"It's not that. You're one of the most studied warriors. But a champion has already been declared," she said in a hoarse voice.

Jake's brows shot up in surprise and he peered behind her.

"Where is he then?" He was expecting to see some monstrous beast Ephyra had found.

"Um," Gabriel cleared his throat and held up his marked hand.

Jake looked at his rival as though he had sprouted tentacles.

"It can't be," he said harshly. "He's not even one of us!"

"He is right now and I need you to train him," Ephyra said firmly.

Jake knew this time she had not chosen a champion, she'd chosen the man she loved. He turned to survey Gabriel, swimming around him and inspecting his tail. Gabriel remained still, but his eyes never left the merman.

"You know nothing of this war."

"You annoyed my tail is bigger than yours?" he snorted as Jake whipped around and splayed his fins.

Gabriel's fins were indeed slightly larger than Jake's and he had no retort.

"I'm her bodyguard."

"I'm her champion." Gabriel leveled him with a solid stare. "If this is your decision, then I have no more to do here," Jake said to Ephyra and bowed.

"It is my decision, but I still have need of you. Of all of you," she addressed the mermen as well. They floated at attention and listened intently.

"Gabriel is my champion, but he will need training. I would have your help."

"You are the last hope we have, princess," Horatio said and bowed, as did the mermen behind him.

"Thank you."

Jake remained stonily silent, his hands in loose fists. Ephyra went over to him and put a hand on his shoulder to lead him away from prying ears.

"I need you," she said softly. He tried to mask his hurt pride with a tight smile.

"I should have told you when I knew I loved you," he said repentantly. "It's too late now."

"Jake, I won't apologize for loving him. I am sorry for not seeing how you felt sooner. Please, give me your support."

The silence was deafening. Jake heard the authority in her voice, as a true princess should sound. She was ready to rule and he couldn't destroy her only chance of avenging her parents.

He turned to her and gently touched her face with his hand, stroking it like he'd done since they were merlings.

"I would have done anything for you, Ephyra. But this is one thing I would refuse," he paused. "You must order me to do this, properly."

"You know Gabriel and I won't be together after this," she said harshly, her eyes blazing.

"And you would still not choose me."

Ephyra squared her shoulders, having nothing to say to that. Jake knew he was the only one she could trust to give Gabriel the tools to succeed. She moved closer to the army of mermen and Gabriel. He could already see her decision and his heart tried to accept it.

"I am commanding Jahyl to begin Gabriel's training immediately. You're to help in any exercises required, and we have only two days before the fight. He will be ready by the night of the sixth day," Ephyra backed no argument.

Jake nodded stiffly and the mermen all bowed once more. Gabriel went to stand by her and Ephyra held his hand up, showing the mark.

"The champion." The merman saluted him and dropped lower.

Jake bowed his head but his body rigid with irritation. He wondered what it would be like to have an enemy for the rest of his life.

# Chapter Thirty-Nine

"Again!" Jake barked.

Gabriel gritted his teeth but tried the evasive maneuver another time, still not fast enough. The projectile spear, made of wood, splintered as it hit his tail. Gabriel felt mild pain and saw a few scales fall off, flashing silver. He was surprised at how fast the weapon could be used under the water. If he could sweat underwater, he was sure he would be dripping.

"Maybe if you threw it straight I could avoid it," he teased Jake, but the other was not in a laughing mood.

Jake had done what Ephyra asked him to but nothing more. Gabriel was tired of trying to make the merman an ally. He shrugged and concentrated on avoiding the two spears Jake hurled at him. Gabriel found that if he flipped his tail just so, he could avoid the weapons and pivot; much like the fish he saw disappear in a flash.

The guards helped Jake further his torture by surrounding him in a ring of sharp coral knives and Gabriel was instructed to block every thrust. He was good at that, using an incredibly strong piece of sharpened coral. Gabriel thought it didn't hurt that Ephyra watched his practices. What would it be like to remain under the water?

"You should recognize this one," Jake said and handed him the rams' horn gun.

Gabriel smiled and aimed. Spines shot out and decimated the targets yards away. He wondered if such long-range weapons were allowed in the enclosed arena.

"Unfortunately, you won't be able to use it," Jake said with a smirk.

Gabriel raised his brows.

"Was that an attempt at humor, Jake?" he asked, equally snarky.

The merman frowned at him and handed him an object that

resembled a sword except it was light, had no hilt and was corn colored.

"Is this food?" Gabriel guessed to aggravate Jake further.

"Sword. It's made from crushed coral, crab shell, and obsidian. It won't ever break but it can be used against you if you lose it. Fight."

Gabriel wasn't prepared for Jake to brandish a similar sword at him. He felt a punishing whack on his shoulder and pain blossomed. Anger flared hot and ready. He swung back but Jake parried. They fought until Gabriel was used to the weapon and he could wield it with ease. The sword wasn't exactly King Arthur worthy but he liked the lightness of it.

Ephyra came over to him with a colorful platter filled with food. Food, he learned, was a loose definition. Gabriel had a hard time swallowing crab shell but fish, scallops, mollusks and even octopi were tolerable. Gabriel wondered if they could have someone throw a few cheeseburgers into the water once in a while. Turning into a merman was different from being born one.

"You are doing well," she said with a smile. Ephyra watched him taste all the food on the plate. He knew she wanted to help him at any cost, including shielding him from Jake's painful glares.

"Thanks." Gabriel liked that he didn't have to drink under the water. His gills filtered enough in and out all the time so that he was never thirsty.

"Next, I have to teach you to feel your power," Ephyra told him when he was finished.

"Power?" he asked skeptically.

"Magic, energy, life force. In some it is stronger, like in you. Merfolk could not have existed without it. It can help us to be invisible to humans, outwit hungry sharks, establish the laws not unlike the ones Erebos has unleashed."

"Oh, magic," he said thoughtfully. It was a concept that he knew only as a show on stage with a man in a top hat and tails.

"Close your eyes," Ephyra said gently and led him to a rock

that formed a seat.

Gabriel tried to feel something but could only hear the soft hum of the ocean, swishing of fish, the guards nearby mumbling.

"Remember when you found Erebos in my room?" she prompted and he tensed.

"Yes."

"Try to call it back."

Gabriel didn't want the violent image in his mind, but he pictured Ephyra bloody and helpless. A sudden surge of energy filled his veins and he could almost feel his muscles surging with pent up aggression. It felt like lines of electricity pulsed through him and made all his senses sharper. He opened his eyes. The energy stayed with him for a few minutes before fading.

"Yes, bring it back," Ephyra said excitedly.

Gabriel tried to think of nothing, just summon whatever that was so he didn't need to think of Ephyra in danger. The magic raced back to him and nearly bolted from his fingertips. He could feel it waiting like a snake in the grass.

"See that rock?" Ephyra pointed to a large piece of stone to the left and Gabriel nodded. "Try to break it."

Gabriel figured if he commanded several middle school children, he could do this. Sparks of light shot from his fingertips and the boulder splintered into pieces.

He smiled triumphantly at Ephyra and she gave him an impulsive hug. Gabriel saw the sadness in her eyes when she pulled back but didn't comment.

He spent the rest of the afternoon practicing until the currents became so violent everyone took shelter.

"Erebos must be in a bad mood," Ephyra said darkly, looking toward the palace to see black clouds rising from the towers.

"This will be just a fit compared to how angry he'll be when he loses," Gabriel told her confidently. He was still intrigued by the simple biological concept of being half a fish and his mind wasn't centered.

"One more night," Ephyra said bitterly. She took his hand and led him away.

Gabriel followed willingly, marveling that even down here he could feel it was evening. The moon's pull on the tides and currents was stronger here than on land.

"So, how much power is one allowed to use in this fight?" he asked as she led him into a large cave.

"As much as you have."

Gabriel stopped to stare at the beautiful lichens that glowed inside, the reflections creating the illusion the cave was above water. Tiny holes let in the moonlight so that it shafted in sparkles. Moss covered rocks stacked to either side and there was a school of glowing blue fish that circled inside like a disco ball.

"This is beautiful," he said, his eyes roving over every little detail.

"I wanted to have one night alone with you," Ephyra confessed gently. She pulled him to her and folded her tail around herself. Her hair shone in the moonlight and floated softly past her shoulders.

Gabriel sat next to her and tried to fold his tail, too. He ended up falling off the rock seat while Ephyra giggled.

"I'm sure this turns you on," he muttered good naturedly.

"I can't ever repay you," she said and wrapped her tail around his.

"It's been worth it," Gabriel said softly and meant it. "I was just going through the motions of life before I met you, Ephyra. My father's passing is hard still. Do you think I'd get to see my family again?" *Even Marcus*, he thought. He had pretty much left him to deal with Sanchez alone in a hurricane.

Ephyra sighed against him.

"I don't know. I wish I could promise you your life back. I'm sorry," she said and looked up into his eyes.

Their lips met instantly, hungrily. Ephyra rubbed herself against him slowly, agonizingly. Gabriel groaned, wishing he knew how merfolk procreated. He was too embarrassed to ask. Ephyra seemed to sense this and guided his hand to her breasts.

"Some is the same," she whispered and bent his head to suck at her taut nipples. The scales had disappeared. Gabriel complied, licking and nipping.

"We are not the same as humans. Mermaids don't get, what is the word, pregnant?"

Gabriel drew back; suddenly his arousal was not quite as strong. He raised an eyebrow and pursed his lips.

"So, just how do mermaids have babies?" he asked in trepidation, not sure he wanted to know.

"You are afraid to know?" Ephyra asked hesitantly.

"Uh, not so much afraid as I don't think I can deal with any more fish stuff." He grinned.

She smiled back and lifted scales on her tail to show him her pouch full of eggs. Gabriel blanched slightly but tried to smile.

"That's pretty," he said lamely.

"They're just eggs, Gabriel," Ephyra said with a laugh. "I know it is very different from humans but it is the way it's done." She seemed embarrassed now. Gabriel reached out a hand to pull her close again.

"That's a biological lesson I wasn't prepared for."

Gabriel could tell she was embarrassed to have shared so much so he spent the next minutes reassuring her she hadn't.

"We don't procreate like humans," Ephyra told him after a long kiss. Gabriel could feel how odd it was for her to be kissing at all under water. Merfolk were more fish than human in some instances. Gabriel understood her sexual frustration. She'd gone from enjoying a human body to one that was fused together.

"What if I touch you here?" he asked and put a gentle finger inside her pouch. The eggs shifted aside and he found her slick inside, warm and tight. Ephyra gasped in sudden arousal.

"No one's ever done that, merfolk are taught it's sacred and no one but the mermaid releases the eggs," she said huskily. "We only need men to spread their seed over the eggs." She giggled and Gabriel thought he would explode from the small circles she was making with her fingernails on the bulge under the scales on his tail.

"It's really not as impressive as a merman," Gabriel rasped jokingly as she pulled it gently out. Ephyra laughed and guided him toward her pouch.

"Maybe merfolk have been doing this wrong," she said as he slid into her and Gabriel felt his blood ignite with heat. He could feel she was afraid but he fit inside her just as he had when she was human.

After they found shuddering release they curled up together and finally slept. The moonlight streamed on them like spotlights and the schools of fish watched over them.

# Chapter Forty

Five o'clock in the morning. Marcus looked at his watch and couldn't sleep anymore. Thoughts of Gabriel, mermaids and loaded guns swirled in his mind. Jane curled next to him, sleeping restlessly. They were holed up in a stolen car in a deserted beach parking lot. Marcus had tried to get Jane to leave but she'd resolutely stuck with him.

Marcus sighed silently as he thought of Gabriel. He had waited for any information from his brother, but Sanchez was trailing them. He peeled the cardboard shades off one of the car windows. The skies were still gray and billowing clouds threatened storms. At least it wasn't raining. Marcus woke Jane and she sat up as if he'd shot a gun next to her ear.

"Hey, just me," he said and opened the door with a creak.

"Sorry. It's a habit now." Jane smiled apologetically and stretched.

"It might be suicide to go out now but we have to get out of here. Sanchez will have men at the state line so let's get to my boat."

Jane nodded solemnly.

"I trust you."

*

Ephyra woke slowly as if in a dream and found herself enfolded in strong arms. She felt her head resting on a broad, muscled chest and the deep breathing of the man beneath her. She shifted gently and saw Gabriel's sleeping face. His eyes were closed peacefully and his hair was dark under water, swaying in the soft current. He was beautiful but when she saw his merman's tail something felt wrong. She realized she preferred him as a human and not one of her kind. Sadly, she reached up to wake him with a kiss. Gabriel's eyes flew open as he kissed her back.

"Hi," he yawned. He looked up at the light.

Ephyra detached herself from him. It was the last time she could embrace him as a lover.

They left the cave silently and somberly. Gabriel saw the host of guards waiting with Jake outfitted in armor at the front. The waters were in a lull of calm and he could see the spires of the arena in the distance. It was finished.

In just hours, he'd be in the middle of those stones, fighting for his life, for an entire underwater realm. Gabriel let the guards dress him in armor and outfit him with weapons.

Ephyra checked over his form. He wore the bracer with the moonstone securely inside it as well as a hardened torso shield. A waistband held his sword and in his left hand he gripped a shield with the royal sigils as well as those of the champion. She adjusted his bone helmet; his jaw jutted out defiantly. She gazed at him for a moment with her beautiful golden eyes.

Gabriel held her gaze and swept a lock of hair behind her ear affectionately. He pulled the helmet off and bent to kiss her forehead. Ephyra felt shivers run up and down her spine, wanting more. She impulsively pushed up to catch his lips, not caring who saw. Gabriel hugged her tightly, letting the intimate love pass between them. For a moment, her hair ensconced them like a cocoon.

"If . . . will you get word to Marcus for me?" Gabriel asked quietly.

Ephyra nodded into his shoulder and a sob caught in her throat. "You'll see him soon."

Gabriel broke the embrace and headed toward the arena. Ephyra didn't follow, but would take her place above the arena to watch.

Jake trailed behind Gabriel and ushered him into the small alcove in the first entrance to the arena. There were only two entrances, one for each competitor. Gabriel heard the raucous cheering and murmurs of the merfolk gathered. He didn't know how many but it sounded like thousands.

"Good luck. I don't wish you to die today," Jake said formally above the din of the crowd.

"Thanks. I appreciate your instruction, Jake. If I'm not successful, you'll take care of her?" he asked, although it pained him to do so.

Jake nodded somberly. "I always have."

Gabriel put his helmet on and saw that Jake was extending his hand. He took it firmly.

"When the horn sounds don't hesitate," Jake said in parting and Gabriel nodded.

He took a deep breath and mentally shook himself. Weapons hung on his waist comfortably and he swished his tail. The fins were strong, supple and ready for the slightest muscle twitch. Gabriel had confidence in his speed. He heard merfolk arguing and cheering on all sides of the arena.

Then the face that he hated appeared on the platform of rock with Ephyra. It made his skin crawl to see Erebos floating next to her. The warlord had a sallow complexion with long graying hair and a smirk on his pale face.

"Merfolk!" he boomed and the din quieted. Thousands of faces turned to him, some with disdain, some with adoration. "The ancient laws provide entertainment for you this day. Acknowledge the champions that will fight in deadly combat."

A roar went up from the crowd as the two warriors stood in separate shadowed sides. Ephyra stood silent and hard next to him. Her lips were thinned into a line and her eyes fixed on the spot where Gabriel floated.

"Why should the lowest not rule what they have a right to? Do not the lower know real suffering?" Erebos shouted and was met with a roar of approval. "Before the main event, I have a gift for the princess."

Erebos turned to the mermaid with a snide smile. He motioned to his mermen and they emerged from the shadows with a figure hung between them.

Even from their distance, Gabriel could hear Ephyra's gasp as the mermen emerged with an old woman whose face was half covered by her long twisting dark hair, no doubt covering more bruises like the ones exposed. The purple and blue marks extended down to her torso and her tail was tattered. He'd bet money this was Scyllane.

"You have no right," Ephyra shouted angrily.

"A gift to the heathen gods as you would call them. Scyllane consults with the ancient runes, so she will be sent back to them," Erebos answered contemptuously. "I assume command now. If you get it back, you can disband this new addition to the game." He motioned for the executioner. A large merman with a thick piece of hardened coral came forth to stand in front of Scyllane.

Gabriel saw Ephyra try to bolt from her spot but Erebos' strong arm caught her and tugged her back. He'd kill that son of a bitch for ever touching her.

"I would advise staying in your place, princess."

"Scyllane!" Ephyra yelled to the sea witch and she looked up tiredly. Her eyes smiled sadly at the mermaid in acknowledgement.

Gabriel saw the witch was ready for death, but he wasn't. He threw the spear in his hand and the executioner gasped as it hit him square in the stomach. He flew back and lay still. Gabriel swam and caught the witch as she fell.

"You are her champion."

"I am," Gabriel answered with a quick glance at Ephyra to see the relieved expression on her face.

Scyllane reached up to touch his face and Gabriel felt a tremor go through his body. The fire dissolved into energy that simmered beneath the surface of his skin, ready to explode.

"You must win," she whispered in his ear. Gabriel gazed for a moment into her wizened eyes.

"Incompetence!" Erebos motioned his executioner to intervene.

Gabriel felt the swish of current before the executioner's spear whizzed by, slicing an inch from his shoulder. He flipped in a whirl of fins, parried the spear from the executioner's hands and plunged his knife into his throat. The merman choked as blood blossomed around him. He saw Jake carrying the sea witch out of the arena. Gabriel saw Jake's men fighting the other guards.

He addressed the platform where Erebos stood watching with a frown.

"I don't have all damn day!" he shouted to the Dark merman.

Erebos smiled despite his annoyance.

"Bythos!" he called forth his fighter.

Gabriel saw the huge merman emerge from the shadows, twice his size with fins thicker than most redwood trees. The merman had pale blond hair, a beefy face and neck and outfitted with more weapons that Gabriel recognized. His armor was black and had Erebos' sigils on them with stripes of red.

Gabriel saw the first blade of coral spear come at him with the speed of an arrow.

# Chapter Forty-One

"We're being followed," Jane said as she glanced behind them at the other boat.

Marcus swore under his breath. Sanchez had too many eyes out.

"Just hang on. I can try to track them with the fish finder," he said. It was a long shot but Marcus hoped the detector would show him where large shoals of fish were, which might lead him to find Jake. The merman had mentioned something about a war and Marcus figured in a war there had to be a lot of bodies under the water. And when he found Jake, he could find his brother and hope that Ephyra was back where she belonged. He glanced behind; the white boat stayed an inconspicuous distance from them.

Marcus throttled down slightly as the clouds split for a moment and a weak sun shone through, turning the spray of the sea into shattered rainbows. He shielded his eyes through the mist and saw a sliver of black against the sun. Marcus instantly dropped his eyes. Was there supposed to be an eclipse today? The cloud cover hid the sun. The boat bounced on a large wave and the clouds closed back up. He shrugged; it made no difference.

"This is what we knew we were in for," he called to Jane and she nodded, eyeing the dark sky to the west. The waves were steadily growing larger and tossing the speedboat like a toy.

"Just find them and let's lose Sanchez!" Jane came to stand next to him at the wheel. She peered at the fish finder. So far the dots were scarce and only showed badly outlined banks. They weren't out too far, so Marcus throttled back up, taking the waves head on.

"Keep an eye on that boat," Marcus instructed her. He only had his .9mm Sig and he hoped he wouldn't have to use it.

*

The arena was filled with screaming merfolk as Gabriel dodged blow after blow. Bythos was a monster of a merman and for an instant Gabriel wondered how he grew that large. The merman was faster than he appeared though. Twice Gabriel felt blazing nicks on his arms from not moving quickly enough. He was hardly aware of the section of merfolk screaming his name, waving various colors of sea kelp that rippled in the water.

Bythos came at him with a spear that he threw and just as Gabriel dodged it, thrust with his sword. Gabriel felt the blade an inch from his side and gritted his teeth. He countered with a thrust of his tail to propel him quickly and sliced down with the coral sword. True to Jake's word, the coral didn't break or bend. He felt it make fleshy contact and Bythos let out an irritated growl.

Gabriel swam in circles around him, jabbing and parrying as fast as he could. Spurts of blood shot up randomly as they both nicked each other. He felt his sword arm strong and sure as it drove the sword toward Bythos' helmet. The point caught the edge and he swung up, tearing the enemy's armor off his head. Bythos' face was caught in a peevish scowl, scars running the length of the left side of his face. The merman's long hair flew around his head like ropey snakes.

Gabriel swam back for a moment to catch his breath and Bythos charged at him. The big merman used his weight and slammed into Gabriel. The breath left his lungs as he was flung against the stone wall. Gabriel drew his small knife and thrust up into Bytho's ribs but the merman blocked his hand. Gabriel felt the weight crushing him against the stone and tried to push him off. His tail seemed to thrash uselessly as Bythos brought down his fist onto Gabriel's shoulder. Pain flared at the base of his neck and his shoulder went numb. Bythos grabbed him around the neck with one large hand, and with the other, he plunged into Gabriel's abdomen. Grunting, Gabriel doubled over but was pushed upright by the force around his neck.

Bythos whipped out a large black sheet of material and before Gabriel could even guess what he would do with it, he flung it over Gabriel's head. Gabriel gasped as suddenly his breath left him. The material closed the gills on the back of his head and the darkness made him dizzy. He felt a fist slam down on the back of his head and pain shot through his entire body. The gill covers protected them but not from a blow of this magnitude.

Gabriel felt himself sliding down into unconsciousness. He gave one last flick of his tail up to hit the back of Bythos' head. He used the other's tactic by wrapping his fins around Bythos' head and slapping his gills.

Bythos roared in pain and let go. Gabriel clawed at the black material over his head and tore it off. The crowd cheered wildly, the din louder than any football game he'd been to. Gabriel drew oxygen into his lungs again and his vision cleared fast enough for him to dodge Bythos' slashing sword. He flipped his tail and shot above the merman. Bythos tracked him with beady eyes and followed.

They once again danced in a circle around the arena, dodging and parrying each other. Gabriel flicked his tail and slapped Bythos' gills as hard as he could when he circled. The merman was growing frustrated as he snatched at empty water. Bythos finally grunted and looked to a guard at the side of the arena. The guard nodded and threw him a ball of dark brown netting. Gabriel looked toward Jake at his side in exasperation.

"We can have aid?" he shouted at Jake.

Jake threw his hands up and wildly motioned he didn't know. He looked around quickly and threw a spear toward Gabriel. Gabriel glowered at him. A spear was hardly creative. He caught it just as a net covered him.

# Chapter Forty-Two

"They're going to start firing!" Jane's words were hardly out of her mouth when the backside of the boat exploded in shards of wood and water.

They hit the deck hard and Marcus scrambled to get the scuba gear on him and Jane. He gave his Glock to Jane, knowing it would fire even when wet.

Marcus jerked and tugged at the wet suit, scrambling to get it on. He looked back and saw Sanchez's boat flashing fire as bullets careened into the hull. Then, he felt the boat rock with a shudder as depth charges were let loose into the water. A barrage of green flares lit the storming sky and flew into the waves to light a deathly path into the depths.

*

Gabriel saw the flares raining down and it illuminated the net around him. The ropes were made of sharp crushed shell and cut into his skin. He could feel it burning and tried to concentrate on the knife in his right hand. It sliced and hacked at the ropes but for every one he cut it seemed another took its place.

*Use your power*, Ephyra's voice seemed to come to him and Gabriel remembered his other weapon. He focused on the tingling feeling just beneath his skin and to his surprise light shot from all directions, melting the net away and resounding like a clap of thunder. Bythos was thrown back and slammed into the invisible barrier that kept the fighters in the arena.

The crowd of merfolk's attention was turned back to the arena and they cheered as the huge beast roared in pain. Gabriel was aware the power wasn't calm and concentrated like before; it was sweeping through him like a wildfire. He called it forward even if he didn't understand the consequences. Power propelled from his fingers as he stretched them out toward Bythos. White light hit the big merman in the chest and he split open in a cloud of blood and intestines.

The merfolk screamed their delight and rage as pieces of Bythos splattered against the barrier, making it visible in a spray of blood. Gabriel, stunned, lay on the sandy bottom and turned his head to see Erebos fuming at the high platform, the green flare light making his face stand out in stark relief.

"The princess has cheated!" he bellowed. "She has brought humans to fight her battles!"

So that was where the flares had come from, Gabriel thought. He lifted himself up in a sweep of his tail and shot toward Erebos. He nearly face planted into the barrier, his eyes level with Erebos'. The Dark lord looked at him with a grim smile.

"It seems I have underestimated her champion, but enjoy your glory for the few minutes you have it."

The crowd was roaring like thunder, confusion starting riots among them.

"I've won. You keep to the rules, you son of a bitch," Gabriel spat at him. He was aware of depth charges firing into the water and realized someone was on the surface sending bombs down.

"You have cheated," Erebos hissed and lifted a horn to his lips. With a long blow, a wail sounded as if death itself were unleashed.

Ephyra swam to Gabriel, fear in her eyes.

"Marcus is here, on the surface," she said hastily.

"What?" Gabriel shouted.

Suddenly, there was another thunderous clap from another depth charge that seemed to still the water for a moment and everyone was thrown back. When it had passed, some merfolk were unconscious. Erebos fingered the small cut on his forehead in anger.

Erebos grinned as he swam up toward the boats on the surface.

"What's happening?" Gabriel cried to Ephyra. She shook her head.

"I don't know!" she yelled. The barrier between them started to give slightly.

*

*Depth charges,* Marcus thought frantically as he struggled against his captors. *Sanchez brought depth charges.* He vainly sought to get to Jane. Marcus saw bullets flying into the water and then divers in black wet suits came flopping over the side. Marcus and Jane leapt from the boat into the frothing water, better there than impaled on bullets.

Current swept him up and Marcus rode it. His head broke the surface and he saw that swirling clouds were coming together in a clash of fury. Lightning hit the water with the force of godlike hammers and thunder boomed overhead. It was too strong and Marcus felt his regulator torn from his mouth, the straps holding the tanks cut like ribbon.

He saw Ephyra as a blur of dark bubbles coming up toward him and Jane and glanced over his shoulder to see Sanchez bearing down.

## Chapter Forty-Three

Ephyra propelled Marcus and Jane back to the debris from his boat. He saw a man from Sanchez's boat aiming at Jane and plunged over her. Jane was thrown forward, her head knocking on the metal railing. She went unconscious.

He heard men shouting in Spanish, the other boat came alongside and then Sanchez stood over him, a silver gun pointed in his face.

"I have lost enough men to you!" he cursed.

Marcus fixed Sanchez with a glare and then something took his gaze.

"I told you the truth, look behind you," he said with a smirk.

Sanchez turned around and Ephyra blasted him off the side of the boat. She hung on to the railings with one arm and pointed the ram's horn gun at the men with the other. The rounds of poisoned spikes shot through them and they splashed into the water, dead before they could even pull their triggers. Ephyra smiled at Marcus grimly and hoisted herself up on the splintered deck.

"Thanks." Marcus clutched his shoulder with one hand and touched Jane with the other. She was still breathing as rain pelted her face. The boat rocked wildly with the rolling waves.

"Is she okay?"

"Yea, think so," Marcus answered. "Is Gabriel?"

"I don't know, but he wanted me to get you to safety. I'll take her to the other boat, follow. You can't do anything for him here." Ephyra tugged Jane and swam quickly toward Sanchez's boat.

*

Gabriel found himself unable to move as he was propelled toward the Dark merman. Erebos' face wore a murderous scowl and lightning flashed in his eyes. The horn's echo surrounded the merman with a dangerous aura of power.

"Champion, I offer you a deal."

Gabriel regarded him steadily, cocking his head. His fingers clutched the sword but he couldn't move them.

"Why, surprised you lost?"

"I haven't lost," Erebos snapped. "It is you who stands to lose and I offer you a chance to live."

"No thanks." Gabriel glared at him. He felt the power coiling inside him.

"I offer more than slavery, like your precious princess does," he said with a smile.

"Again, no," Gabriel responded coldly.

Erebos frowned at him and then shrugged.

"If that is your choice." He sent electric magic into Gabriel's torso. Gabriel was aware someone was screaming in agony, only to realize it was him. He felt a weakness take him, his mind clouded with darkness.

He saw Erebos put a finger to his temple and close his eyes. All at once Gabriel saw into the other's mind. It was full of chaotic desire, bloody mangled bodies and icy fire cut with magic. He saw a human man kneeling in pain, enslaved.

"You were human," he whispered as the pain shook his core. The sword fell from his hand.

"I was enslaved by these animals and that would be your fate," came his soft hiss. "But no longer."

In his mind Gabriel saw the entire coast being destroyed by funnel clouds of Erebos' fury, rain sleeting down roofs and wind that knocked houses over. Floods began to race as waves rose, summoned by his invisible hand. Gabriel groaned as much from the pain as from the destruction the humans didn't even see coming. He felt another shock of power shake his insides and Gabriel screamed as it tore him.

There was a faint sound as Erebos left his mind. It was a low keening screech and suddenly there was a wave of blue gray shapes surrounding them. Gabriel tried vainly to make his tail work, to keep him afloat but he was falling. He heard Erebos' shout of dismay as blue whales rushed in from all sides.

"Click," Gabriel said with a small smile and then he couldn't see anything.

The whales crashed forward as they battered Erebos' guards and tried to snatch him in their mouths. Erebos blew them back with a blast and a few were blown apart, their flesh floating in chunks to the dark ocean floor.

*Find your strength!* The whale's voice echoed in Gabriel's foggy head as she swept under him, carrying him. Gabriel could taste the blood in the water and his gills opened wider for more oxygen. Slowly, his vision cleared and he tried to sit up. Pain shot through his back and arms. Gabriel saw his fins were torn in places and his chest full of scratches. Click was moving awkwardly now and Gabriel floated off her.

*Thank you, I won't let him hurt you,* he thought and put his hands together.

With a muttered curse, he spied Erebos rocketing toward him. Gabriel let his mind go blank and just felt the energy. The power convulsed once and then he was spinning up, light shooting from his fingertips. He hit Erebos but the other twisted in time so only his shoulder was scalded. Gabriel lashed out with white light, Erebos countered with green. They circled, locked in a battle of will.

Gabriel felt a jolt hit his tail and growled. He shot back and saw Erebos' left fin disappear. Light shot in every direction and time collapsed. Erebos sent a beam straight toward the bracer. He had glimpsed the blue moonstone.

Gabriel felt his forearm explode in pain and the bracer fell from his wrist. He frantically grabbed for it but it was blasted away with another green shaft of light. He turned tail and raced for the shore. Gabriel knew it would take a few minutes for the change to come and he pushed his body as fast as it could go. Out here, he would drown in seconds. He could feel Erebos behind him, enjoying the race.

Gabriel felt his lungs start to burn as his gills folded into his head. He tried not to panic as he flashed his tail harder, propelling him toward land. The water suddenly started to make him sluggish; he used his arms now to help swim. With a thump, he felt his tail turn into human legs. Gabriel pumped them with all his strength but knew it wouldn't be enough. He let himself float to the surface, his head broke through the waves and he saw the beach in the distance. It was too far. Gabriel felt his heart sink and with it, he was pulled down under the water.

Erebos leered at him under the water as he held him. Gabriel didn't even try to struggle; he just glared for all he was worth. Then, he felt Erebos' hold break as a spear came catapulting into the dark lord's left shoulder. The merman cried out, clutching the shaft that protruded. He yanked it out with a snarl.

Jake rammed into the dark lord with all his speed and tried to slice him with his sword. He missed and barely dodged Erebos' green blast at his tail. He didn't stop for the pain as he grabbed Gabriel and hauled him to the surface. Gabriel gulped air gratefully and then felt himself being pulled swiftly toward shore. Jake grabbed around his middle and with a jump start like a cannon they hurtled toward the beach. Gabriel could only hold on as he tried not to choke on the salt water.

There was a concussive blast and Gabriel felt himself being launched out of the water. He landed painfully on churning sand and saw Jake's unconscious form a few feet away, the waves surging around him. Gabriel sent him a silent thank you as he scrambled toward him. He spied a pair of shorts snagged on a piece of driftwood. He thanked God someone had littered. His legs were shaky but he clambered up the beach.

Erebos' tall, lean figure rose out of the waves. Gabriel saw him changing, human legs gathering beneath him as he stood shrouded in a black cloak that stuck to him like spines. He walked confidently out of the water, the waves parting for him and the sand giving him firm footing.

"It seems you've run out of friends, champion," Erebos said with a sneer.

"My name is Gabriel."

Gabriel stood and walked away from Jake, trying to draw the dark lord's attention away from him. He felt the wind battering him like a ram and was nearly knocked over. Erebos laughed.

"Pathetic even in your rightful form," he said and cast his hands out further. Rain pelted Gabriel and lightning struck at his feet. Gabriel felt the impact as he jumped aside. Thunder followed, so loud it hurt his ears.

Gabriel searched quickly for anything to help him but there was nothing, just the wide expanse of deserted beach that was being ravaged by the storm. Erebos stood in the middle of it, his hair whipping around his calm face.

Gabriel crouched into fighting stance. If he was to die after everyone had placed their faith in him, it would be on his terms.

Erebos tossed his head.

## Chapter Forty-Four

Ephyra curled her tail around Scyllane's body and cradled her head in her lap. The sea witch's eyes were a cloudy blue and her breath came in ragged gasps. Ephyra looked around at Erebos' guards but they were talking among themselves. They finally made up their minds and fifty of them went to assist their master. Only a dozen stayed behind, watching the princess.

Ephyra ignored them. She wished Jake were there but he'd disappeared. She concentrated on trying to stem the blood from Scyllane's wounds.

"I have overlooked one thing, merling," Scyllane said hoarsely.

"Shhh, you did wonderfully. I didn't understand why you put me in the human realm, but I need to thank you for that," she said softly.

Scyllane smiled faintly.

"I never intended what happened. No reason to thank me." All her rage, all the hate was boiling down to one last breath. She coughed and bubbles came out from her mouth. Ephyra put a soothing hand on her forehead.

Ephyra couldn't feel Gabriel anymore and feared the worst. His spirit was no longer in the water.

"You should not doubt love as I did," Scyllane told her scornfully. Ephyra was surprised at her tone.

"I . . ." she began but the truth was she had already given up. "You're right, but I can't feel him anymore." Tears welled in her eyes. She hadn't wanted to face it until now, in the stillness of the deep.

"The moon will overtake the sun soon," the sea witch whispered and closed her eyes.

"What?" Ephyra asked, wondering what this had to do with love.

Scyllane had gone silent and still. Ephyra closed her eyes in sorrow and knelt over her, her shoulders trembling. She placed her hand on the sea witch's heard.

"Be at peace."

An object, glistening gold came to rest on the sea witch's body. Ephyra picked it up and examined the mirror. It was a small handheld mirror that gave back Ephyra's haggard reflection. The mirror started to vibrate and suddenly the surface came to life. Ephyra gasped as she saw first the cloud banks, billowing and shielding the sun. The image took her far above the clouds to where the sun shone on the white tops. She peered closer and saw a dark sliver beginning to cross the sun's orb. With a gasp, she heard Scyllane's words. *The moon would cross the sun.* Ephyra stared spellbound at what the mirror showed her.

*

Gabriel danced in the sand around Erebos, his fists lashing out and missing. The dark lord in his human form was quick, his body evasive. The storm swirled around them and Gabriel could hardly keep the rain out of his eyes. Sweat smeared over his body as he tried to hit his target.

"When you tire of this, I will be happy to oblige you in an extended death," Erebos said as he circled. His fist shot out and Gabriel countered it with his forearm. He struck out a leg and caught the man behind his knee. Erebos grunted in reluctant surprise but righted himself.

Gabriel didn't answer but concentrated. He felt his legs shaking and knew it wouldn't be long before fatigue got the better of him. They grappled with fists, legs and kicks in the sand that sucked his feet down. Waves began to get higher and Gabriel had to dodge them, moving up further on the beach. He turned, irate, at the distraction and cursed the waves. To his surprise, they receded as if pulled back by a string.

Gabriel panted and rained down blow after blow, satisfied he was finally hitting solid flesh. The man beneath him lashed out and he reeled back, his face burning. Gabriel threw himself right back at him and they collapsed in pile of thrashing limbs. Erebos kneed him in the stomach; Gabriel grunted and slammed his elbow down on the other's bad shoulder. Green light flashed angrily from the merman.

Gabriel felt something in his grasp, a control that was heady and almost as if he was holding the reins to the wind itself. He could feel the lightning, hot and white and feel the rain as it lashed his body. He commanded it to stop and the rain lessened. Gabriel glanced skyward, his lips twisted in a curious smile. He looked over to see Erebos firing a green ball of fire at him. Gabriel called lightning to strike it before it reached him.

"Trouble?" he called to the dark lord.

Erebos glided toward the water and shot bolt after bolt at Gabriel. He deflected them all and Erebos muttered curses under his breath. This was impossible. The power of the storms was his. He let waves break against his legs, hoping the ocean would restore his control. Instead, Gabriel made the waves rise up against him and he found himself on his back in the sand.

For a moment, the clouds parted as Gabriel told the storm to relax. They both felt soft rays of sun on their faces and saw the black shadow crossing the sun. Gabriel raised his eyebrows. He felt the pull of the eclipse like static charging through him.

He saw several heads pop up above the water and recognized the guards. Gabriel clenched his hand into a fist and with it, the water tightened around them. The mermen shouted in alarm and looked to Erebos for help. He tried to stretch out his hand but all it caused was a frothing of waves. Gabriel thrust them onto the sand where they flopped angrily.

"Seems your friends are in trouble."

The dark lord glowered at him. In fury, Erebos gathered

all he had left and launched himself at Gabriel. The flash of blazing green and gold light blasted into Gabriel and he felt himself pushed back by the force as if he were up against a wall. He managed to keep his feet and held both hands out to catch the power surge. He felt searing pain on his already beaten body but power surged through him.

White light caught Erebos' vicious face as he slashed at Gabriel's throat. The power cut Erebos' head cleanly off his shoulders and Gabriel fell back, the water closing over his head. He asked the water to hold him up and it surrounded him like a blanket. Gabriel saw Erebos' still form float away on the current, his mouth gaping in death.

The waves gently deposited him back on the sand and Gabriel sat wearily, his legs trembling. He surveyed the still mermen who lay on the sand, unable to move.

"Your master is dead. Serve the Coral house now and swear your loyalty or follow him to the depths," Gabriel shouted. The men all yelled oaths back at him, their eyes sincere. Gabriel lifted his hand and the waves took the merman back into the water. He watched as they disappeared beneath the water.

Gabriel lay back and felt the power fading as the shadow left the sun. The clouds gathered but their rain was soft now, the thunder a distant rumble. Gabriel thought of Ephyra and his heart contracted. He had done his duty and he waited for fins to regrow around his legs. The champion had won, he was now a slave. At the least, he would make sure all were loyal to her.

When all he heard was the patter of rain and felt nothing but his calf muscles clenching he gathered energy to sit up. His legs were still there, no scales. Gabriel heard a soft groaning and saw Jake holding his head, his tail half way in the water. Gabriel walked over to him and flopped down. The merman gave him a rueful smile.

"Saw the end of the show. That was impressive," he said and his tail flipped.

"Thanks. Don't ask where it came from, I have no idea," Gabriel said lightly. He smiled at Jake. The two sat in silence as the rain washed the blood from their faces.

## Chapter Forty-Five

Ephyra followed the mirror, the formations of rock and sand in the reflection were the same on either side of her. She swam away from the palace, away from the arena. The mirror suddenly showed her the darkness in a crevice. She took a deep breath and plunged into the pit. The mirror lit up like a star and guided her path under the volcanic rocks. Ephyra felt the temperature dropping and an odd sensation of claustrophobia as she squeezed through tunnels of stone.

At last the tunnel opened into a large cavernous space. Strange worms glided over the walls and small, eyeless fish that looked like glass sifted through the sandy bottom. Ephyra looked around at the oblong obsidian structures that sat, three across in the middle of the space. They pulsed with a purple glow and there were sigils written all over them.

The mirror reflected the three stones and then Ephyra saw again the darkened sun. The mirror heated in her hand and urgently she felt it pull toward the stones. Ephyra saw a small hole opening up at the base of the middle stone, the tallest. Purple and green symbols began to glow brighter as she took the mirror toward them. The opening was a perfect fit for the handle of the mirror and called to it, pulling the mirror toward it like a siren.

A blast like thunder with no sound made her dart back. The stone began to hum, the pressure increased in the chamber. Ephyra saw the mirror spinning in the hole, its gold light sparking like a jellyfish.

The mirror stopped spinning and in its glass, she saw Scyllane's peaceful face, restored to her former glory. The mermaid smiled faintly.

"Destroy the runes, princess. Under a blue moon is the only time you will have the power to set him free." The sea witch disappeared.

Ephyra experimentally grabbed the mirror to see if she could pull it out. However, when she tried the stone began to crack. Ephyra let out a breath. Destroy the stones. She placed both hands on the mirror and cranked it every way, making the stone tremble and groan as pieces fell apart. The sigils gave a scream that sounded almost human as their light faded from them. Ephyra gasped and pulled harder, the mirror grew hot. Finally, the stone broke into dust and the two on either side fell to rubble.

She floated back and watched the mirror explode into thousands of sparkling fragments. The eyeless fish ate the particles as they got in their way. The walls of the chamber went dark and Ephyra was lost in it. She only heard the faint scrabbling of the fish and crabs and her erratic breathing. Ephyra groped blindly in the dark for the opening she'd come through.

There was a huge, piercing shaft of white and purple light that suddenly erupted from the black stones. Ephyra saw the opening and darted in to it just as the rocks began to quiver. The magic shot out of the chamber like javelins and shattered the stones. Ephyra swam quickly, scraping her hands and tail on the rocks as she made for the end of the tunnel.

The opening was close and Ephyra pushed hard to get out. She shot away from the crumbling tunnels and only stopped to glance back. White light was spiraling up to the surface in a funnel of bubbles and what looked like ancient shapes, old merfolk. Ephyra swam away, feeling an immense relief but tinged with sadness. She could let Gabriel go now but she found she didn't want to.

*

Jake cocked his head at the distant white light that blasted from the foaming waters and lit up the dark clouds like reverse lightning.

"Did you do that?"

"No," Gabriel said, staring at the column of light that seared through the cloud bank. Lightning seemed to be attracted to it and the whole thing went up in a blaze of fire.

"What was that about? Did he come back?" Gabriel half joked.

"I don't think so," Jake said uncertainly.

Ephyra's head popped up above the waves and they both gasped in happiness. Gabriel found his feet and plunged into the water to encircle her in his arms. She returned his hug as they fell into the waves.

"You won, you did it," she said hardly able to speak. Gabriel didn't have words either, so he took her face in his hands and plunged down to kiss her. Then, he drew back quickly.

"We can't do this anymore, can we?" he said bitterly and let his hands fall away.

Ephyra bit her lip. She smiled through her tears.

"I released you. You're free." She tried to sound happy.

Gabriel regarded her for a tense moment.

"What do you mean, released me?"

"The sun," she motioned to the blackened orb. "It's now blue. A blue moon. The one time when the runes could be destroyed. You won't be a slave or a merman," Ephyra told him and gave him a playful shove.

Gabriel let it move him back. He wasn't sure why his heart was tearing and why he wasn't happy he was keeping his legs. He searched Ephyra's eyes to see if this was what she wanted but she had turned to Jake for distraction.

"Jake!" Ephyra exclaimed and went to embrace her friend. The merman hugged her tightly and flopped his way into the deeper water. Gabriel felt waves slapping his thighs, but he was frozen in place.

"Thank you more than you know, Gabriel," Ephyra turned to him and he sank down into the water so he was eye level with her. The mist sprayed his hair black and Ephyra had to swallow hard at his chiseled, familiar face. She had to resist the urge to give him the stone again and come with her. He belonged here.

"I wish I could repay you," she started, but he cut into her gratitude angrily.

"I didn't do this for anyone but you. And now you want nothing to do with me?"

Gabriel saw she was trying hard not to cry and somehow he didn't care at the moment. "I thought you'd be happier where you belong and not with me," she said softly. Jake quietly slipped under the water.

"You have to take care of Marcus and your mother. I have too much responsibility here. I just thought it was the best solution and you wouldn't be bound to me."

Gabriel's lips thinned. His anger fueled all the energy he had left. *I am bound to you by more than a simple law, I thought you felt the same,* he thought but banished it. She was right though, they had no life together. A realm needed its ruler. He couldn't smile but he didn't want to leave with like this.

"Thank you for my freedom," Gabriel said tightly and brushed her hair from her face.

Ephyra pulled herself toward him but Gabriel didn't move toward her.

"I can still see you, right? We can meet at night along the shore . . . I love you," Ephyra blurted.

"Of course," he lied. Gabriel felt his chest suffocating and he needed to get out of the water.

*I love you,* he thought but couldn't say it.

Ephyra slipped under the waves and he saw her tail wave farewell. He stood, the water rushing around his legs and the sand swirling at his feet. Gabriel sluggishly made his way toward shore. He spread his toes on hard packed sand, remembering how it felt to have fins instead. He sighed as he heard the sound of a motor boat. Gabriel turned to see his brother waving and the white boat bouncing on calm waters. The rain was lessening even more.

Gabriel walked along the shore toward the docks. He couldn't feel his feet, couldn't feel his body. All he felt was loss and it consumed him like a drowning man.

# Chapter Forty-Six

"This is amazing," Marcus declared and lifted his margarita to toast Jane and Gabriel. They were sitting on Tortola, the sun shining on the wreckage of the coast but shining nonetheless. He'd bought two condos and he'd insisted Gabriel have the one with the best view. The white balcony overlooked the spectacular ocean, crescent white beach and the distant other islands.

The following two weeks after the storm, they'd laid low but discovered no one missed drug dealers too much. Marcus had gone back to the warehouse and club, declaring Sanchez's operation over. The men disappeared into the grimy cracks of the city and Marcus was left with nearly a million dollars. After careful consideration. they'd decided no one would believe the money was left after Sanchez was killed by sea monsters and mermaids. Marcus had declared it his and offered to give Gabriel half. His brother, the enigma he was, declined except for a new car and airfare home.

"It's been a trip all right," Jane said, her blue eyes sparkling. She sipped her drink and cast a worried glance at Gabriel. He'd been sketchy on the details but told them the merfolk were safe. He hadn't so much as mentioned Ephyra.

A day later, sitting in silence, Gabriel stared at the shifting blues of the water before him. He wondered if she were out there, wondering where he was.

Marcus came out to the balcony, cleared his throat and shoved the plate of food toward his brother. Jane followed him with margaritas.

"Better eat before you leave. You sure you don't want to stay a while?"

Gabriel shifted his attention to his brother.

"I need to get back. Mom's been going crazy," he said, ignoring the chilled shrimp.

"I was thinking we should come up for Christmas this year." Marcus smiled at Jane. She returned it with a giggle.

"She'd like that."

Gabriel was glad his brother was maturing. He smiled as best he could. His thoughts of home led him to rethink his career. Gabriel didn't want to go back to the classroom, the crowded halls, the academic headache or the grading. He leaned back and knew where he wanted to be but it was impossible.

"We're going to take a walk tonight, if you want to come," Marcus said and took a gulp of his margarita. "Turtles should be coming up or maybe we'll hear the whales again."

Gabriel smiled, again for appearance sake. He remembered a certain whale that'd saved his life. He wished he could talk to her again. The humid air suddenly seemed to close in his lungs. There would be no more beach walking for him.

# Chapter Forty-Seven

The whales voices filled Gabriel's head on the entire plane ride back, the car ride to his place, and even as he unpacked. The swell of the ocean seemed to follow him even in the whisper of the trees. The tow company had brought his car back and he was grateful to see it hadn't been covered in vandalism. He'd sell it for as much as it was worth. The Lexus he had now more than sufficed.

The only thing that distracted him was Dag when he picked up the dog from the sitter. The yellow ball of fur licked him furiously and seemed determined not to let him out of his sight this time. Gabriel sat with the dog on the couch, listlessly watching TV for hours on end. He took him on long runs but even that didn't deplete the energy in his mind. Gabriel found nights were the worst. He couldn't find rest and his mind kept running the last week in his head as if it were his only memory.

The cold breeze of fall had settled over the city and already Christmas decorations were beginning to be sold in stores. Gabriel put in his notice to the college and didn't feel any regret the next day. He felt a weight lifted from his chest, actually.

One sleepy, gray afternoon Gabriel woke to the sound of his cell phone. Sleep came to him in patches of time. He turned over and saw it was his mother's number. He ignored it pulling the pillow over his head. Dag snored on the ground next to the bed.

Gabriel felt as if something dark had aimed for his heart but just missed it, keeping him alive to suffer. Instead the pain was all consuming and never ending. Erebos was just a shadow now in his dreams. Gabriel wondered if the circumstances hadn't collided if he'd have beaten the dark lord. But the possibilities all resulted in the same outcome. Ephyra was gone.

Unable to fall back to sleep, Gabriel got up and did something he never did. He took a bath. He filled the tub with hot water and sank into the soapy warmth, letting it cover his head. He tried to feel gills on the back of his head, willing them to come. When his lungs burned and he was on the verge of passing out he came up for air. This was stupid and Gabriel cursed himself for the thought. He dried off and just as he was apathetically picking a shirt to wear, Dag barked.

The dog took off at a hopping run toward the door. Gabriel passed on a shirt and went to open the door. He was dismayed to see Kim, her blond hair fluffed and her sweater tight. She took in his bare chest with wide, hungry eyes and a smile.

"I thought you might like this," she purred and held out a casserole. "Your mom has been worried about you."

Gabriel saw a flash of red.

"You spoke with my mother?"

Kim seemed taken aback by his tone and nervously smoothed her sweater. It swelled over the nice curves of her body but she could have been naked and Gabriel wouldn't have cared.

"Well, I had been worried since you've been gone so long and I called her," Kim explained.

"I see. Thanks for this," Gabriel said and took the dish. He walked to the kitchen to put it in the fridge. Out of the corner of his eye, he saw Kim sidle inside the door.

"So, I was thinking if you wanted to go out to dinner with me and some friends tonight you're welcome. I mean, I know I made you dinner, but Sark's is supposed to be better than a chicken casserole . . ."

Gabriel listened with half an ear.

"I'm afraid he's engaged tonight," a commanding voice came from behind him and Gabriel froze. That voice reverberated through his core and he felt his throat choking

"Who are you?" Kim asked.

Gabriel turned and his body started to shake. Ephyra stood in the doorway dressed in a long brown coat and boots. Her raven's wing hair glistened and fell around luminous gold eyes. Kim was giving her a distinctive laser glare, sizing up the other woman. Gabriel barely registered Kim as he stared at Ephyra and her sweet, if a bit regal, smile. She was just the way he remembered her on two legs, a little unsure but seemed to float just the same.

"Can I come in?" Ephyra asked teasingly and Kim smirked.

"Yea," Gabriel managed and then shook himself. "Kim, this isn't a good time." He couldn't help the grin breaking out on his face as his neighbor exited, her nose in the air.

Ephyra came toward him and as if in a dream, he ran to her and picked her up in his exuberance. She smelled of the sweetness of the sea. Her hair tangled in his face and Gabriel crushed her in his arms. He finally set her down but didn't release her.

"Do you need the champ already?" he joked and saw her smile. Her face was so familiar but it felt as if he hadn't seen her in years.

Ephyra grinned and shook her head.

"I just love you."

Gabriel circled her in his arms and kissed her head. He couldn't stand not being closer to her but any closer and he'd squeeze the breath from her.

"I love you," he whispered next to her ear. He felt her pull back and there were tears in her eyes.

"I want to live with you for as long as you'll have me," she said tremulously. "The weeks without you have been miserable and I've been no help to my people. I will stay human with you for as long as you need me."

She opened her coat to reveal the blue moonstone hanging on a silver chain around her neck.

Gabriel also saw that she wore a tank top with no bra and shorts underneath it. That was his woman, no sense of human clothing at all.

"I would have you forever," was all he said before descending on her mouth and touching her lips.

Ephyra melted into him as he held her, stripping off her coat and then leading her toward his room. She kicked the cumbersome boots off and moaned at his touch. Gabriel used every part of his body, his hands, his mouth, to let her know how much he loved her.

They loved each other for hours until at last they collapsed on the bed exhausted. Ephyra fingered the stone thoughtfully and sighed contentedly. Gabriel folded his hand over hers and the stone.

"What happens now? Who's running your realm?" he asked with a wry smile.

"Jake and Muriel," Ephyra giggled. "They were both more than happy to take over. I think the merfolk need to see humans aren't the enemy we think they are. We're hoping to set up an alliance, with your help of course."

"Sounds like a job." Gabriel kissed her swollen lips. He didn't think he'd ever tire of feeling their softness.

"If we could work together maybe the oceans would thrive instead of being depleted."

"If anyone can get this done it's you and a certain champion. I would still like to retain my title," he teased and she kissed him to shut him up.

Gabriel cupped her face in his hands.

"Does this mean I can marry you?" he asked seriously.

"Well, I didn't come back to be your mistress," she said with a grin. He laughed and enfolded her in his arms.

"As long as the stone remains on me I'll be human. After five years I will need to make a decision where I want to stay," she explained and Gabriel nuzzled her ear.

"And what would I have to do to convince you to stay?" he asked huskily. Her kiss answered nothing but this for a lifetime.

## About the Author

Emily Bourne is a pen name for the author who resides in the Midwest with her husband and a Lab/pit mix who likes to sit on her feet while she writes. She followed her love of words and art to a bachelor's degree in English, a minor in art, and has always had a passion for story telling since she was old enough to write. She loves the natural world and likes to combine that with supernatural twists.

You can find her on Facebook or on her blog *www.rainingpaint.wordpress.com/*, she would love the company!

In the mood for more Crimson Romance? Check out *Wicked Paradise* by Erin Richards at *CrimsonRomance.com*.

www.ingramcontent.com/pod-product-compliance
Lightning Source LLC
Chambersburg PA
CBHW010639100726
47900CB00011B/2886

* 9 7 8 1 4 4 0 5 5 5 7 6 3 *